DI SIONE'S
VIRGIN MISTRESS

BY

SHARON KENDRICK

MILLS & BOON

First published in Great Britain 2016
By Mills & Boon, an imprint of HarperCollins*Publishers*
1 London Bridge Street, London, SE1 9GF

Large Print edition 2017

Special thanks and acknowledgement are given to Sharon Kendrick for her contribution to the The Billionaire's Legacy series.

ISBN: 978-0-263-07065-1

DI SIONE'S
VIRGIN MISTRESS

For Sarah-Jane Volkers, who will know exactly why this book is dedicated to her when she reads it!

And to the brilliant Rafael Vinoly, whose words painted such a perfect vignette of Long Island life…

CHAPTER ONE

DANTE DI SIONE FELT the adrenaline pumping through his body as he walked into the tiny airport terminal. His heart was pounding and his forehead was beaded with sweat. He felt like he'd been running. Or just rolled away from a woman after a bout of particularly energetic sex. Even though it was a long time since he could even remember *having* sex. He frowned. How long?

His mind raced back over the past few weeks spent chasing across continents and flitting in and out of different time zones. He'd visited a dizzying array of countries, been presented with a whole shoal of red herrings and wandered up against several dead ends before arriving here, in the Caribbean. All in pursuit of a priceless piece of jewellery which his grandfather wanted for reasons he'd declined to share. Dante felt the tight clench of his heart. A dying man's wish.

Yet wasn't the truth that he had been tantalised by the task he'd been given and which he had taken on as a favour to someone who had given him so much? That his usually jaded appetite had been sharpened by a taste of the unusual. Truth was, he was dreading going back to his high-octane world of big business and the slightly decadent glamour of his adopted Parisian home. He had enjoyed the unpredictability of the chase and the sense that he was stepping outside his highly privileged comfort zone.

His hand tightened around the handle of his bag which contained the precious tiara. All he needed to do now was to hang on to this and never let it go—at least, not until he had placed it at his grandfather's sickbed so that the old man could do what he wanted with it.

His mouth felt dry. He could use a drink, and… something else. Something to distract him from the fact that the adrenaline was beginning to trickle from his system, leaving him with that flat, empty feeling which he'd spent his whole life trying to avoid.

He looked around. The small terminal was filled with the usual suspects which this kind of upmarket Caribbean destination inevitably attracted. As well as the overtanned and ostentatiously wealthy, there seemed to have been some photo shoot taking place, because the place was full of models. He saw several giraffe-tall young women turn in his direction, their endless legs displayed in tiny denim shorts and their battered straw hats tilted at an angle so all you could see were their cute noses and full lips as they pouted at him. But he wasn't in the mood for anyone as predictable as a model. Maybe he'd just do a little work instead. Get on to René at his office in Paris and discover what had been going on in his busy and thriving company while he'd been away.

And then his gaze was drawn to a woman sitting on her own. The only pale person in a sea of tanned bodies. Her hair was blond and she looked as fragile as spun sugar—with one of those pashmina things wrapped around her narrow shoulders which seemed to swamp her. She looked *clean*. He narrowed his eyes. Like she'd spent most of her life underwater and had just been brought up to the surface. She was sitting at the bar with an untouched glass of pink champagne in front of her, and as their eyes met, she picked up her glass, flustered, and began to stare at it as if it contained the secret to the universe—though he noticed she didn't drink any.

Was it that which made him start walking towards her, bewitched by a sudden demonstration of shyness which was so rare in the world he inhabited? With a few sure strides he reached her and put his bag down on the floor, right next to a remarkably similar brown leather carry-on. But then she lifted her head and all he could think about was the fragile beauty of her features.

'Hi,' he said.

'Hi,' she said in a very English accent as she blinked up at him through thick lashes.

'Have we met before?' he questioned.

She looked startled. Like someone who had been caught in an unexpected spotlight. She dug her teeth into her lower lip and worried them across the smooth rosy surface.

'I don't think so,' she said, then shook her head so that the strands of fair hair shimmered over her narrow shoulders like a silky cascade of water. 'No, we haven't. I would have remembered.'

He leaned on the bar, and smiled. 'But you were staring at me as if you knew me.'

Willow didn't answer—not straight away—her head was too full of confusion and embarrassment combined with a powerful tug of attraction which she wasn't quite sure how to handle. Yes, *of course* she had been staring at him because—quite honestly—who wouldn't?

Beneath the pashmina, she felt the shiver of goose bumps as she met his mocking gaze, acknowledging that he was probably the most perfect man she'd ever seen—and she worked in an industry which dealt almost exclusively with perfect men. Dressed with the carelessness only the truly wealthy could carry off, he looked as if he'd only just fallen out of bed—though probably not his own. Faded jeans clung to unbelievably muscular thighs, and although his silk shirt was slightly creased, he still managed to convey a sense of power and privilege. His eyes were bright blue, his black hair was tousled and the gleam of his golden olive skin hinted at a Mediterranean lineage. Yet behind the brooding good looks she could detect a definite touch of steel—a dangerous edge which only added to his allure.

And Willow was usually left cold by good-looking men, something she put down to a certain shyness around them. Years of being ill, followed by a spell in an all-girls school, had meant that she'd grown up in an exclusively female environment and the only men she'd ever really met had been doctors. She'd been cocooned in her own little world where she'd felt safe—and safety had been a big deal to her.

So what was it about this man with the intense

blue eyes which had made her heart start slamming against her ribcage, as if it was fighting to get out of her chest?

He was still looking at her questioningly and she tried to imagine what her sisters would say in similar circumstances. They certainly wouldn't be struck dumb like this. They'd probably shrug their gym-honed shoulders and make some smart comment, and hold out their half-empty glasses for a refill.

Willow twisted the stem of the champagne glass in between her finger and thumb. *So act like they do. Pretend that gorgeous-looking men talk to you every day of the week.*

'I imagine you must be used to people staring at you,' she said truthfully, taking her first sip of champagne and then another, and feeling it rush straight to her head.

'True.' He gave a flicker of a smile as he slid onto the bar stool beside her. 'What are you drinking?'

'No, honestly.' She shook her head, because

surely the champagne must be responsible for the sudden warmth which was making her cheeks grow hot. 'I mustn't have too much. I haven't eaten anything since breakfast.'

He raised his eyebrows. 'I was going to ask if it was any good.'

'Oh. Yes. Of course. Right. Silly of me. It's…' Feeling even more flustered, Willow stared at the fizzing bubbles and drank a little more, even though suddenly it tasted like medicine on her tongue. 'It's the best champagne I've ever had.'

'And you often drink champagne on your own at airports, do you?' he drawled.

She shook her head. 'No. Actually, I'm celebrating the end of a job.'

Dante nodded, knowing this was his cue to ask her about her job, but the last thing he wanted was to have to listen to a résumé of her career. Instead, he asked the bartender for a beer, then leaned against the bar and began to study her.

He started with her hair—the kind of hair he'd like to see spread over his groin—because although he wouldn't kick a brunette or a redhead out of bed in a hurry, he was drawn to blondes like an ant to the honeypot. But up close he could see anomalies in her appearance which made her looks more interesting than beautiful. He noted the almost-translucent pallor of her skin which was stretched over the highest cheekbones he'd ever seen. Her eyes were grey—the soft, misty grey of an English winter sky. Grey like woodsmoke. And although her lips were plump, that was the only bit of her which was—because she was thin. Too thin. Her slim thighs were covered in jeans onto which tiny peacocks had been embroidered, but that was as much as he could see because the damned pashmina was wrapped around her like an oversize tablecloth.

He wondered what had drawn him towards her when there were other more beautiful women in the terminal who would have welcomed his company, rather than looking as if a tiger had suddenly taken the seat beside her. Was it the sense that she didn't really fit in here? That she appeared to be something of an outsider? And hadn't he always been one of those himself? *The man on the outside who was always looking in.*

Maybe he just wanted something to distract him from the thought of returning to the States with the tiara, and the realisation that there was still so much which had been left undone or unsaid in his troubled family. Dante felt as if his grandfather's illness had brought him to a sudden crossroads in his life and suddenly he couldn't imagine the world without the man who had always loved him, no matter what.

And in the meantime, this jumpy-looking blonde was making him have all kinds of carnal thoughts, even though she still had that wary look on her face. He smiled, because usually he let women do all the running, which meant that he could walk away with a relatively clear conscience when he ended the affair. Women who chased men had an inbuilt confidence which usually appealed to him and yet suddenly the novelty of someone who was all tongue-tied and flustered was really too delicious to resist.

'So what are you doing here?' he questioned, taking a sip of his beer. 'Apart from the obvious answer of waiting for a flight.'

Willow stared down at her fingernails and wondered how her sisters would have answered *this*. Her three clever, beautiful sisters who had never known a moment of doubt in their charmed lives. Who would each have doubtless murmured something clever or suggestive and had this gorgeous stranger tipping back his dark head and laughing in appreciation at their wit. They certainly wouldn't have been sitting there, tying themselves up in knots, wondering why he had come over here in the first place. Why was it only within the defining boundaries of the work situation that she was able to engage with a member of the opposite sex without wishing that the floor would open up and swallow her?

This close, he was even more spectacular, with a raw and restless energy which fizzed off him like electricity. But it was his eyes which were truly remarkable. She'd never seen eyes like them. Bluer than the Caribbean sky outside. Bluer even than the wings of those tiny butterflies which used to flutter past on those long-ago summer evenings when she'd been allowed to lie outside. A bright blue, but a hard blue—sharp and clear and focused. They were sweeping over her now, their cerulean glint visible through their forest of dark lashes as he waited for her answer.

She supposed she should tell him about her first solo shoot as a stylist for one of the UK's biggest fashion magazines, and that the job had been a runaway success. But although she was trying very hard to feel happy about that, she couldn't seem to shake off the dread of what was waiting for her back in England. Another wedding. Another celebration of love and romance which she would be attending on her own. Going back to the house which had been both refuge and prison during her growing-up years. Back to her well-meaning sisters and overprotective parents. Back to the stark truth that her real life was nowhere near as glamorous as her working life.

So make it glamorous.

She'd never seen this man before and she was unlikely to see him again. But couldn't she—for once in her life—play the part which had always been denied to her? Couldn't she pretend to be passionate and powerful and *desirable*? She'd worked in the fashion industry for three years now and had watched professional models morph into someone else once the camera was turned on them. She'd seen them become coquettish or slutty or flirtatious with an ease which was breathtaking. Couldn't she pretend that this man was the camera? Couldn't she become the person she'd always secretly dreamed of being, instead of dull Willow Hamilton, who had never been allowed to do *anything* and as a consequence had never really learned how to live like other women her age?

She circled the rim of the champagne glass with her forefinger, the unfamiliar gesture implying—she *hoped*—that she was a sensual and tactile person.

'I've been working on a fashion shoot,' she said.

'Oh.' There was a pause. 'Are you a model?'

Willow wondered if she was imagining the brief sense of *disappointment* which had deepened his transatlantic accent. Didn't he like models? Because if that was the case, he really *was* an unusual man. She curved her lips into a smile and discovered that it was easier than she'd thought.

'Do I look like a model?'

He raised his dark eyebrows. 'I'm not sure you really want me to answer that question.'

Willow stopped stroking the glass. 'Oh?'

His blue eyes glinted. 'Well, if I say no, you'll pout and say, *Why not?* And if I say yes, you'll still pout, and then you'll sigh and say in a weary but very affected voice, *Is it that obvious?*'

Willow laughed—and wasn't it a damning indictment of her social life that she should find herself shocked by the sound? As if she wasn't the kind of person who should be giggling with a handsome stranger at some far-flung spot of the globe. And suddenly she felt a heady rush of freedom. And excitement. She looked into the mocking spark of his eyes and decided that she could play this game after all. 'Thank you for answering me so honestly,' she said gravely. 'Because now I know I don't need to say anything at all.'

His gaze became speculative. 'And why's that?'

She shrugged. 'If women are so unoriginal that you can predict every word they're going say, then you can have this conversation all by yourself, can't you? You certainly don't need me to join in!'

He leaned forward and slanted her a smile in response and Willow felt a sense of giddy triumph.

'And that would be my loss, I think,' he said softly, his hard blue eyes capturing hers. 'What's your name?'

'It's Willow. Willow Hamilton.'

'And is that your real name?'

She gave him an innocent look. 'You mean Hamilton?'

He smiled. 'I mean Willow.'

She nodded. 'It is—though I know it sounds like something which has been made up. But it's a bit of a tradition in our family. My sisters and I are all named after something in nature.'

'You mean like a mountain?'

She laughed—*again*—and shook her head. 'A bit more conventional than that. They're called Flora, Clover and Poppy. And they're all very beautiful,' she added, aware of the sudden defensiveness in her tone.

His gaze grew even more speculative. 'Now you expect me to say, *But you're very beautiful, too*.' His voice dipped. 'And you respond by…'

'And I told you,' interrupted Willow boldly, her heart now pounding so hard against her ribcage that she was having difficulty breathing, 'that if you're so astute, you really ought to be having this conversation with yourself.'

'Indeed I could.' His eyes glittered. 'But we

both know there are plenty of things you can do on your own which are far more fun to do with someone else. Wouldn't you agree, Willow?'

Willow might not have been the most experienced person on the block where men were concerned and had never had what you'd call a *real* boyfriend. But although she'd been cosseted and protected, she hadn't spent her life in *total* seclusion. She now worked in an industry where people were almost embarrassingly frank about sex and she knew exactly what he meant. To her horror she felt a blush beginning. It started at the base of her neck and rose to slowly flood her cheeks with hot colour. And all she could think about was that when she was little and blushed like this, her sisters used to call her the Scarlet Pimpernel.

She reached for her glass, but the clamp of his hand over hers stopped her. Actually, it did more than stop her—it made her skin suddenly feel as if it had developed a million new nerve endings she hadn't realised existed. It made her glance down at his olive fingers which contrasted against the paleness of her own hand and to think how perfect their entwined flesh appeared. Dizzily, she lifted her gaze to his.

'Don't,' he said softly. 'A woman blushing is a rare and delightful sight and men like it. So don't hide it and don't be ashamed. And—just for the record—if you drink more alcohol to try to hide your embarrassment, you're only going to make it worse.'

'So you're an expert on blushing as well as being an authority on female conversation?' she said, aware that his hand was still lying on top of hers and that it was making her long for the kind of things she knew she was never going to get. But she made no attempt to move her own from underneath and wondered if he'd noticed.

'I'm an expert on a lot of things.'

'But not modesty, I suspect?'

'No,' he conceded. 'Modesty isn't my strong point.'

The silence which fell between them was broken by the sound of screaming on the other side of the terminal and Willow glanced across to see a child bashing his little fists against his mother's thighs. But the mother was completely ignoring him as she chatted on her cell phone and the little boy's hysteria grew and grew. *Just talk to him*, thought Willow fiercely, wondering why some people even bothered *having* children. Why they treated the gift of birth so lightly.

But then she noticed that Blue Eyes was glancing at his watch and suddenly she realised she was missing her opportunity to prolong this conversation for as long as possible. Because wouldn't it be great to go home with the feeling of having broken out of her perpetual shyness for once? To be able to answer the inevitable question, *So, any men in your life these days, Willow?* with something other than a bright, false smile while she tried to make light of her essentially lonely life, before changing the subject.

So ask him his name. Stop being so tongue-tied and awkward.

'What's your name?' asked Willow, almost as if it was an afterthought—but she forced herself to pull her hand away from his. To break that delicious contact before he did.

'Dante.'

'Just Dante?' she questioned when he didn't elaborate further.

'Di Sione,' he added, and Willow wondered if she'd imagined the faint note of reluctance as he told her.

Dante took a sip of his beer and waited. The world was small, yes—but it was also fractured. There were whole groups of people who lived parallel existences to him and it was possible that this well-spoken young Englishwoman who blushed like a maiden aunt wouldn't have heard of his notorious family. She'd probably never slept with his twin brother or bumped into any of his other screwed-up siblings along the way. His heart grew cold as he thought about his twin, but he pushed the feeling away with a ruthlessness which came easily to him. And still he waited, in case the soft grey eyes of his companion suddenly widened in recognition. But they didn't. She was just looking at him in a way which made him want to lean over and kiss her.

'I'm trying to imagine what you're expecting my response to be,' she said, a smile nudging the edges of her lips. 'So I'm not going to do the obvious thing of asking if your name is Italian when clearly it is. I'm just going to remark on what a lovely name it is. And it is. Di Sione. It makes me think of blue seas and terracotta roofs and those dark cypress trees which don't seem to grow anywhere else in the world except in Italy,' she said, her grey eyes filling with mischief. 'There. Is that a satisfactory response—or was it predictable?'

There was a heartbeat of a pause before Dante answered. She was so *unexpected*, he thought. Like finding a shaded space in the middle of a sizzling courtyard. Like running cool water over your hot and dirty hands and seeing all the grime trickle away. 'No, not especially predictable,' he said. 'But not satisfactory either.'

He leaned forward and as he did he could smell the tang of salt on her skin and wondered if she'd been swimming earlier that morning. He wondered what her body looked like beneath that all-enveloping shawl. What that blond hair would look like if it fell down over her bare skin. 'The only satisfactory response I can think of right now is that I think you should lean forward and part your lips so that I can kiss you.'

Willow stared at him—shocked—as she felt the whisper of something unfamiliar sliding over her skin. Something which beckoned her with a tantalising finger. And before she had time to consider the wisdom of her action, she did exactly as he suggested. She extended her neck by a fraction and slowly parted her lips so that he could lean in to kiss her. She felt the brush of his mouth against hers as the tip of his tongue edged its way over her lips.

Was it the champagne she'd drunk, or just

some bone-deep *yearning* which made her open her mouth a little wider? Or just the feeling of someone who'd been locked away from normal stuff for so long that she wanted to break free. She wanted to toss aside convention and not be treated like some delicate flower, as she had been all her life. She didn't want to be Willow Hamilton right then. She wanted the famous fairy godmother to blast into the Caribbean airport in a cloud of glitter and to wave her wand and transform her, just as Willow had been transforming models for the past week.

She wanted her hair to stream like buttery silk down her back and for her skin to be instantly tanned, shown to advantage by some feminine yet sexy little dress whose apparent simplicity would be confounded by its astronomical price tag. She wanted her feet to be crammed into sky-high stilettos which still wouldn't be enough to allow her to see eye to eye with this spectacular man, if they were both standing. But she didn't want to be standing—and she didn't want to be sitting on a bar stool either. She wanted to be lying on a big bed wearing very sexy underwear and for those olive fingers to be touching her flesh again—only this time in far more intimate spots as he slowly unclothed her.

All those thoughts rushed through her mind in just the time it took for her own tongue to flicker against his and Willow's eyes suddenly snapped open—less in horror at the public spectacle she was making of herself with a man she'd only just met than with the realisation of what was echoing over the loudspeaker. It took a full five seconds before her befuddled brain could take in what the robotic voice was actually saying, and when it did, her heart sank.

'That's me. They're calling my flight,' she said breathlessly, reluctantly drawing her mouth away from his, still hypnotised by the blazing blue of his eyes. With an effort she got off the stool, registering the momentary weakness of her knees as she automatically patted her shoulder bag to check her passport and purse. She screwed up her face, trying to act like what had happened was no big deal. Trying to pretend that her breasts weren't tingling beneath her pashmina and that she kissed total strangers in airports every day of the week. Trying not to hope that he'd spring to his feet and tell her he didn't want her to go. But he didn't.

'Oh, heck,' she croaked. 'It's the last call. I can't believe I didn't hear it.'

'I think we both know very well why you didn't hear it,' he drawled.

But although his eyes glinted, Willow sensed that already he was mentally taking his leave of her and she told herself it was better this way. He was just a gorgeous man she'd flirted with at the airport—and there was no reason why she couldn't do this kind of thing in the future, if she wanted to. It could be the springboard to a new and exciting life if she let it. That is, if she walked away now with her dignity and dreams intact. Better that than the inevitable alternative. The fumbled exchange of business cards and the insincere promises to call. Her waiting anxiously by the phone when she got back to England. Making excuses for why he hadn't rung but unable—for several weeks at least—to acknowledge the reason he hadn't. The reason she'd known all along—that he was way out of her league and had just been playing games with her.

Still flustered, she bent down to grab her carry-on and straightened up to drink in his stunning features and hard blue eyes one last time. She tried her best to keep her voice steady. To not give him any sense of the regret which was already sitting on the horizon, waiting to greet her. 'Goodbye, Dante. It was lovely meeting you. Not a very original thing to say, I know—but it's true. Safe journey—wherever you're going. I'd better dash.'

She nearly extended her hand to shake his before realising how stupid that would look and she turned away before she could make even more of a fool of herself. She ended up running for the plane but told herself that was a good thing, because it distracted her from her teeming thoughts. Her heart was pounding as she strapped herself into her seat, but she was determined not to allow her mind to start meandering down all those pointless *what if* paths. She knew that in life you had to concentrate on what you had, and not what you really wanted.

So every time she thought about those sensual features and amazing eyes, she forced herself to concentrate on the family wedding which was getting closer and the horrible bridesmaid dress she was being made to wear.

She read the in-flight magazines and slept soundly for most of the journey back to England, and it wasn't until she touched down at Heathrow and reached into the overhead locker that she realised the carry-on bag she'd placed in the overhead locker wasn't actually *her* bag at all. Yes, it was brown, and yes, it was made of leather—but there all similarities ended. Her hands began to tremble. Because this was of the softest leather imaginable and there were three glowing gold initials discreetly embossed against the expensive skin. She stared at it with a growing sense of disbelief as she matched the initials in her head to the only name they could stand for, and her heart began to pound with a mixture of excitement and fear.

D.D.S.
Dante Di Sione.

CHAPTER TWO

DANTE'S PLANE WAS halfway over northern Spain when he made the grim discovery which sent his already bad mood shooting into the stratosphere. He'd spent much of the journey with an erection he couldn't get rid of—snapping at the stewardesses who were fussing and flirting around him in such an outrageous way that he wondered whether they'd picked up on the fact that he was sexually excited, and some hormonal instinct was making them hit on him even more than usual.

But he wasn't interested in those women in too-tight uniforms with dollar signs flashing in their eyes when they looked at him. He kept thinking about the understated Englishwoman and wondered why he hadn't insisted she miss her flight, so that he could have taken her on board his plane and made love to her. Most women couldn't resist sex on a private jet, and there was no reason she would be any different.

His mouth dried as he remembered the way she had jumped up from the bar stool like a scalded cat and run off to catch her flight as if she couldn't wait to get away from him. Had that ever happened to him before? He thought not.

She hadn't even asked for his business card!

Pushing her stubbornly persistent image from his mind, he decided to check on his grandfather's precious tiara, reaching for his bag and wondering why the old man wanted the valuable and mysterious piece of jewellery so much. Because time was fast running out for him? Dante felt the sudden painful twist of his heart as he tried to imagine a future without Giovanni, but he couldn't get his head around it. It was almost impossible to envisage a life without the once strong but still powerful figure who had stepped in to look after him and his siblings after fate had dealt them all the cruellest of blows.

Distracted by the turbulent nature of his thoughts, he tugged at the zip of the bag and frowned. He couldn't remember it being so full because he liked to travel light. He tugged again and the zip slid open. But instead of a small leather case surrounded by boxer shorts, an unread novel and some photos of a Spanish castle he really needed to look at for a client before his next meeting—it was stuffed full of what looked suspiciously like…

Dante's brows knitted together in disbelief. *Swimwear?*

He looked at the bag more closely and saw that instead of softest brown leather embossed with *his* initials, this carry-on was older and more battered and had clearly seen better days.

Disbelievingly, he began to burrow through the bikinis and swimsuits, throwing them aside with a growing sense of urgency, but instantly he knew he was just going through the motions and that his search was going to be fruitless. His heart gave a leap in his chest as a series of disastrous possibilities occurred to him. How ironic it would be if he'd flown halfway across the globe to purchase a piece of jewellery which had cost a king's ransom, only to find that he'd been hood-winked by the man who had sold it to him.

But no. He remembered packing the tiara himself, and although he was no gem expert, Dante had bought enough trinkets as pay-offs for women over the years to know when something was genuine. And the tiara *had* been genuine—of that he'd been certain. A complex and intri-cate weaving of diamonds and emeralds which had dazzled even him—a man usually far too cynical to be dazzled.

So where the hell was it now?

And suddenly Dante realised what must have happened. Willow—*what the hell had been her surname?*—must have picked up his bag by mis-take. The blonde he'd been so busy flirting with at the airport, that he'd completely forgotten that he was carrying hundreds of thousands of dol-lars' worth of precious stones in his hand luggage. He'd been distracted by her misty eyes. He'd read in them a strange kind of longing and he'd fed her fantasy—and his own—by kissing her. It had been one of those instant-chemistry moments, when the combustion of sexual attraction had been impossible to ignore, until the last call for her flight had sounded over the loudspeaker and broken the spell. She'd jumped up and grabbed her bag. Only she hadn't, had she? She'd grabbed *his* bag!

He drummed his fingers on the armrest as he considered his options. Should he ask his pilot to divert the plane to London? He thought about his meeting with the Italian billionaire scheduled for later that evening and knew it would be both insulting and damaging to cancel it.

He scowled as he rang for a stewardess, one of whom almost fell over herself in her eagerness to reach him first.

'What can I get for you, sir?' she questioned, her eyes nearly popping out of her head as she looked at the haphazard collection of swimwear piled in the centre of the table.

Dante quickly shoved all the bikinis back into the bag, but as he did so, his finger hooked on to a particularly tiny pair of bottoms. He felt his body grow hard as he felt the soft silk of the gusset and thought about Willow wearing it. His voice grew husky. 'I want you to get hold of my assistant and ask him to track down a woman for me.'

The stewardess did her best to conceal it, but the look of disappointment on her face was almost comical.

'Certainly, sir,' she said gamely. 'And the woman is?'

'Her name is Willow Hamilton,' Dante ground out. 'I need her number and her address. And I need that information by the time this plane lands.'

There were four missed calls on her phone by the time Willow left the Tube station in central

London, blinking as she emerged into the bright July sunshine. She stepped into the shadow of a doorway and looked at the screen. All from the same unknown number and whoever it was hadn't bothered to leave a voicemail. But she knew who the caller must be. *The sexy stranger. The man she'd kissed. The blue-eyed man whose carry-on she had picked up by mistake.*

She felt the race of her heart. She would go home first and then she would ring him. She wasn't going to have a complicated conversation on a busy pavement on a hot day when she was tired and jet-lagged.

She had already made a tentative foray inside, but the bag contained no contact number, just some photos of an amazing Spanish castle, a book which had won a big literary prize last year and—rather distractingly—several pairs of silk boxer shorts which were wrapped around a leather box. She'd found her fingertips sliding over the slippery black material of the shorts and had imagined them clinging to Dante Di

Sione's flesh and that's when her cheeks had started doing that Scarlet Pimpernel thing again, and she'd hastily stuffed them back before anyone on the Heathrow Express started wondering why she was ogling a pair of men's underpants.

She let herself into her apartment, which felt blessedly cool and quiet after the heat of the busy London day. She rented the basement from a friend of her father's—a diplomat in some far-flung region whose return visits to the UK were brief and infrequent. Unfortunately one of the conditions of Willow being there was that she wasn't allowed to change the decor, which meant she was stuck with lots of very masculine colour. The walls were painted bottle-green and dark red and there was lots of heavy-looking furniture dotted around the place. But it was affordable, close to work and—more importantly—it got her away from the cloying grip of her family.

She picked up some mail from the mat and went straight over to the computer where she tapped in Dante Di Sione's name, reeling a little to discover that her search had yielded over two hundred thousand entries.

She squinted at the screen, her heart beginning to pound as she stared into an image which showed his haunting blue eyes to perfection. It seemed he was some sort of mega entrepreneur, heading up a company which catered exclusively for the super-rich. She looked at the company's website.

We don't believe in the word impossible.
Whatever it is you want—we can deliver.

Quite a big promise to make, she thought as she stared dreamily at photos of a circus tent set up in somebody's huge garden, and some flower-decked gondolas which had been provided to celebrate a tenth wedding anniversary party in Venice.

She scrolled down. There was quite a lot of stuff about his family. Lots of siblings. *Snap*, she thought. And there was money. Lots of that. A big estate somewhere in America. Property in

Manhattan. Although according to this, Dante Di Sione lived in Paris—which might explain why his accent was an intriguing mix of transatlantic and Mediterranean. And yet some of the detail about his life was vague—though she couldn't quite put her finger on why. She hadn't realised precisely what she'd been looking for until the word *single* flashed up on the screen and a feeling of satisfaction washed over her.

She sat back and stared out at the pavement, where from this basement-level window she could see the bottom halves of people's legs as they walked by. A pair of stilettos tapped into view, followed by some bare feet in a pair of flip-flops. Was she really imagining that she was in with a chance with a sexy billionaire like Dante Di Sione, just because he'd briefly kissed her in a foreign airport terminal? Surely she couldn't be *that* naive?

She was startled from her daydream by the sound of her mobile phone and her heart started beating out a primitive tattoo as she saw it was the same number as before. She picked it up with fingers which were shaking so much that she almost declined the call instead of accepting it.

Stay calm, she told herself. *This is the new you. The person who kisses strangers at airports and is about to start embracing life, instead of letting it pass her by.*

'Hello?'

'Is that you, Willow?'

Her heart raced and her skin felt clammy. On the phone, his transatlantic/Mediterranean twang sounded even more sexy, if such a thing was possible. 'Yes,' she said, a little breathlessly. 'It's me.'

'You've got my bag,' he clipped out.

'I know.'

The tone of his voice seemed to change. 'So how the hell did that happen?'

'How do you think it happened?' Stung into defence by the note of irritation in his voice, Willow gripped the phone tightly. 'I picked it up by mistake...*obviously.*'

There was a split-second pause. 'So it wasn't deliberate?'

'Deliberate?' Willow frowned. 'Are you serious? Do you think I'm some sort of thief who hangs around airports targeting rich men?'

There was another pause and this time when he spoke the irritation had completely vanished and his voice sounded almost unnaturally composed. 'Have you opened it?'

A little uncomfortably, Willow rubbed her espadrille toe over the ancient Persian rug beneath the desk. 'Obviously I had to open it, to see if there was any address or phone number inside.'

His voice sounded strained now. 'And you found, what?'

Years of sparring with her sisters made Willow's response automatic. 'Don't you even remember what you were carrying in your own bag?'

'You found, *what*?' he repeated dangerously.

'A book. Some glossy photos of a Spanish

castle. And some underpants,' she added on a mumble.

'But nothing else?'

'There's a leather case. But it's locked.'

At the other end of the phone, Dante stared at the imposing iron structure of the Eiffel Tower and breathed out a slow sigh of relief. Of course it was locked—and he doubted she would have had time to get someone to force it open for her even if she'd had the inclination, which he suspected she didn't. There had been something almost *otherworldly* about her...and she seemed the kind of woman who wouldn't be interested in possessions—even if the possession in question happened to be a stunning diadem, worth hundreds of thousands of dollars.

He could feel the strain bunching up the muscles in his shoulders and he moved them slowly to release some of the tension, realising just how lucky he'd been. Or rather, how lucky *she* had been. Because he'd been travelling on a private jet with all the protection which came with own-

ing your own plane, but Willow had not. He tried
to imagine what could have happened if she'd
been stopped going through customs, with an
undeclared item like that in her possession.

Beads of sweat broke out on his forehead and
for a moment he cursed this mission he'd been
sent on—but it was too late to question its le-
gitimacy now. He needed to retrieve the tiara as
soon as possible and to get it to the old man, so
that he could forget all about it.

'I need that bag back,' he said steadily.

'I'm sure you do.'

'And you probably want your swimwear.' He
thought about the way his finger had trailed over
the gusset of that tiny scarlet bikini bottom and
was rewarded with another violent jerk of lust
as he thought about her blond hair and grey eyes
and the faint taste of champagne on her lips. 'So
why don't I send someone round to swap bags?'

There was a pause. 'But you don't know where
I live,' she said, and then, before he had a chance
to reply, she started talking in the thoughtful tone

of someone who had just missed a glaringly obvious fact. 'Come to think of it—how come you're ringing me? I didn't give you my phone number.'

Dante thought quickly. Was she naive enough not to realise that someone like him could find out pretty much anything he wanted? He injected a reassuring note into his voice. 'I had someone who works for me track you down,' he said smoothly. 'I was worried that you'd want your bag back.'

'Actually, you seem to be the one who's worried, Mr Di Sione.'

Her accurate tease stopped him in his tracks and Dante scowled, curling his free hand into a tight fist before slowly releasing his fingers, one by one. This wasn't going as he had intended. 'Am I missing something here?' he questioned coolly. 'Are you playing games with me, Willow, or are you prepared to do a bag-swap so that we can just forget all about it and move on?'

In the muted light of the basement apartment, Willow turned to catch a glimpse of her shadowed features in an antique oval mirror and was suddenly filled with a determination she hadn't felt for a long time. Not since she'd battled illness and defied all the doctors' gloomy expectations. Not since she'd fought to get herself a job, despite her family's reluctance to let her start living an independent life in London. She thought about her sister Clover's wedding, which was due to take place in a few days' time, when she would be kitted out in the hideous pale peach satin which had been chosen for the bridesmaids and which managed to make her look completely washed out and colourless.

But it wasn't just that which was bothering her. Her vanity could easily take a knock because she'd never really had the energy or the inclination to make her looks the main focus of her attention. It was all the questions which would inevitably come her way and which would get worse as the day progressed.

So when are we going to see you walking down the aisle, Willow?

And, of course, the old favourite: *Still no boyfriend, Willow?*

And because she would have been warned to be on her best behaviour, Willow would have to bite back the obvious logic that you couldn't have one without the other, and that since she'd never had a proper boyfriend, it was unlikely that she would be heading down the aisle any time soon.

Unless…

She stared at her computer screen, which was dominated by the rugged features of Dante Di Sione. And although he might have been toying with her—because perhaps kissing random women turned him on—he had managed to make it feel *convincing*. As if he'd really *wanted* to kiss her. And that was all she needed, wasn't it? A creditable performance from a man who would be perfectly capable of delivering one. Dante Di Sione didn't have to be her real boyfriend—he just had to look as if he was.

'Don't I get a reward for keeping your bag safe?' she questioned sweetly.

'I'll buy you a big bunch of flowers.'

'Flowers make me sneeze.'

'Chocolates, then.'

'I'm allergic to cocoa.'

'Stop playing games with me, Willow,' he snapped. 'And tell me what it is you're angling for.'

Willow stared at the piercing blue eyes on the computer screen. His thick black hair looked as if he had been running his fingers through it and she remembered how it had felt to have his lips brushing over hers. It was now or never. It was all about seizing the moment and doing something you wouldn't normally do. Because what was the point of sitting back and moaning about your fate as if it was set in stone, instead of trying to hammer out something new for yourself?

And here was a chance staring her straight in the face.

She drew in a deep breath. 'What I want won't cost you anything but your time. I'm being a bridesmaid at my sister's wedding next weekend and I'm fed up with people asking me why I don't have a boyfriend. All you have to do is pretend to be that man. For one day only, you will be my fictitious but very convincing boyfriend, Mr Di Sione. Do you think you could manage that?'

CHAPTER THREE

HE SHOULD HAVE told her no. Should have told her that he hated weddings. Because marriage stood for everything he despised and distrusted. Lies and deception and manipulation.

Dante straightened the silver-grey tie which complemented his formal charcoal suit and stared at his reflection in the hotel mirror.

So why *hadn't* he said no? Why *had* he agreed to accompany Willow Hamilton to her sister's wedding, where she was being a bridesmaid? It was true that she had his grandfather's tiara in her possession and she had been demonstrating a not-very-subtle form of blackmail to get him to be her plus one. But Dante was not a man who could be manipulated—and certainly not by a woman. If he'd really wanted that tiara back he would have gone straight round to her apartment and *taken* it—either by reason or seduction or quiet threat—because he nearly always got what he wanted.

So why hadn't he?

He gave his tie one final tug and watched as his reflected face gave a grim kind of smile.

Because he wanted her? Because she'd interested and intrigued him and awoken in him a sexual hunger he'd been neglecting these past weeks?

The reflected smile intensified.

Well, why not?

He picked up his car keys and went outside to the front of the hotel, where the valet was opening the door of the car he'd hired for the weekend. It was an outrageously fast car—a completely over-the-top machine which would inevitably attract the attention of both men and women. And while it wouldn't have been Dante's first choice, if Willow wanted him to play the part of a very rich and super-keen lover, then it followed that he ought to drive something which looked like everyone's idea of a phallic substitute.

He drove through the streets of central London and tooted the horn as he drew up outside Willow's basement apartment. She appeared almost immediately and he watched her walk towards him, narrowing his eyes with instinctive appraisal—because she looked... He swallowed. She looked *incredible*. Gone was the big pashmina which had shielded her from the airport's overzealous air conditioning and hidden most of her body. In its place was a pale dress which skimmed the tiniest waist he'd ever seen, its flouncy skirt swirling provocatively around her narrow knees. Her blond hair was plaited and Dante felt his mouth dry. As she grew closer he could see that the collar of her dress was embroidered with tiny daisies, and it made her look as if she'd been picked fresh from a meadow that morning. She looked ethereal and fragile and he couldn't seem to tear his eyes away from her.

He shook his head slightly as once again he acknowledged her fey beauty and the realisation that she didn't seem quite part of this world.

Certainly not *his* world. And then he noticed that she was carrying nothing but a small suitcase.

'Where's my carry-on?' he demanded as he got out of the car to take the case from her.

There was a pause as she met his gaze. 'It will be returned to you after the deal is done.'

'After the deal is done?' he echoed softly.

'When the wedding is over.'

He raised his eyebrows at her mockingly, but made no attempt to conceal the sudden flicker of irritation in his voice. 'And if I insist on taking it now? What then?'

He saw a momentary hesitation cross her fragile features, as if she had suddenly realised just who it was she was dealing with. But bravado won the day and she shot him an almost defiant look which made him want to pin her over the bonnet of the car and kiss her senseless.

'You're not in a position to insist, Dante,' she said, sliding inside with a graceful movement which made him wish she could do it again, in slow motion. 'I have something you want and you have to pay for it.'

He switched on the engine and wondered if she was aware that she had something else *he* wanted, and that by the end of the day he would have taken it… 'So where are we going?' he said.

'My family home. It's in Sussex. I'll direct you.'

'Women are notoriously bad at directions, Willow—we both know that. So why don't you just give me the postcode and I can program it into the satnav?'

She turned to look at him, a frown creasing her brow. 'Are you for real, or did you just complete a crash course in being patronising? I think I can just about find my way to my family home without needing a robot to guide me.'

'Just don't fall asleep,' he warned.

'I'll do my best. But you're not exactly an aid to relaxation, are you?' Settling back in her seat, she gave him a clear list of instructions, then waited until he had negotiated his way out of London towards the south, before she asked, 'So what's in the bag which makes you want it so much?'

'Boxer shorts.' He shot her a look. 'But you already know that.'

Willow didn't react, even though the mention of his boxer shorts was threatening her with embarrassment, which she suspected was his intention. Because this was the new Willow, wasn't it? The woman who had decided to take control of her own destiny instead of having it decided by other people. The woman who was going to live dangerously. She studied his rugged profile as he stared at the road ahead. 'A few items of underwear wouldn't usually be enough to get a man like you to take a complete stranger to a family wedding and pretend to be her boyfriend.'

'Let's get a couple of things straight, shall we, Willow? Firstly, I have no intention of discussing the contents of that bag with you,' he said as he powered the car into the fast lane. 'And secondly, I intend to play your *lover*—not your damned *boyfriend*—unless your looks are deceiving and you happen to be fifteen.'

'I'm twenty-six,' she said stiffly.

'You look much younger.'

'That's what everyone says.'

There was a pause. 'Is that a roundabout way of telling me I'm unoriginal?'

She shrugged. 'Well, you know what they say… if the cap fits…'

A reluctant smile curved the edges of his lips. 'You need to tell me something about yourself before we get there,' he said. 'If you're hoping to convince people we're an item.'

Willow stared out of the car window as they drove through the sun-dappled lanes, and as more and more trees appeared, she thought about how much she loved the English countryside. The hedgerows were thick with greenery and in the fields she could see yellow and white ox-eye daisies and the purple of snake's head frit-illary. And suddenly she found herself wishing that this was all for real and that Dante Di Sione was here because he wanted to be, not because she was holding him to ransom over some mystery package.

She wondered how much to tell him. She didn't want him getting scared. She didn't want him to start treating her as if she was made of glass. She was worried he'd suddenly start being *kind* to her if he learned the truth, and she couldn't stand that. He was rude and arrogant and judgemental, but she rather liked that. He wasn't bending over backwards to please her—or running as fast as he could in the opposite direction, which was the usual effect she had on people once they knew her history.

His words interrupted her silent reverie.

'We could start with you explaining why you need an escort like me in the first place,' he said. 'You're a pretty woman. Surely there must be other men who could have been your date? Men who know you better than I do and could have carried off a far more convincing performance.'

She shrugged, staring at the toenails which were peeping through her open-toed sandals— toenails which had been painted a hideous shade of peach to match the equally hideous bridesmaid dresses, because Clover had said that she wanted her sisters to look like 'a team.'

'Maybe I wanted to take someone who nobody else knew,' she said.

'True,' he agreed. 'Or you could—and I know this is controversial—you could always have chosen to attend the wedding on your own. Don't they say that weddings are notoriously fertile places for meeting someone new? You might have got lucky. Or are you one of those women who believes she isn't a complete person unless she has a man in tow?'

Willow couldn't believe what he'd just said. Had she really thought his rudeness was charming? Well, scrub that. She found herself wishing she'd asked around at the magazine to see if anyone there could have been her guest. But most of the men she worked with were gay—and the place was a hotbed of gossip. It wouldn't have done her image much good if she'd had to trawl around for a suitable escort, because the biggest sin you could commit in the fashion industry was to admit to being lonely.

She sneaked a glance at Dante. Whatever his shortcomings in the charm department he was certainly a very suitable escort—in every sense of the word. The formality of his pristine two-piece looked just as good against his glowing olive skin as the faded denim jeans had done. Perhaps even more so. The made-to-measure suit hugged his powerful body and emphasised its muscularity to perfection—making her shockingly aware of his broad shoulders and powerful thighs. The slightly too long black hair appeared more tamed than it had done the other day and suddenly she found herself longing to run her fingers through it and to muss it up.

She felt a rush of something molten tugging at the pit of her belly—something which was making her wriggle her bottom restlessly against the seat. Did she imagine the quick sideways glance he gave her, or the infuriatingly smug smile which followed—as if he was perfectly aware of the sudden aching deep inside her which was making it difficult for her to think straight.

She licked her lips. 'I'm not really like my sisters,' she began. 'You remember I'm one of four?'

'I remember.'

'They've always had millions of boyfriends, and I haven't.'

'Why not?'

He shot the question at her and Willow wondered if now was the time for the big reveal. To tell him how ill she'd been as a child. To tell him that there had been times when nobody had been sure if she would make it. Or to mention that there were residual aspects of that illness which made her a bad long-term choice as a girlfriend.

But suddenly her attention was distracted by the powerful interplay of muscles as he tensed one taut thigh in order to change gear and her mouth dried with longing. No, she was not going to tell him. Why peddle stories of her various woes and make herself look like an inevitable victim in his eyes? Today she was going to be a different Willow. The kind of Willow she'd always wanted to be. She was going to embrace the way he was making her feel, and the way he was making her feel was…*sexy.*

Carelessly, she wriggled her shoulders. 'I've been too wrapped up in my career. The fashion world can be very demanding—and competitive. I've been working at the magazine since I left uni, and they work you very hard. The swimwear shoot I was doing in the Caribbean was my first big break and everyone is very pleased with it. I guess that means I'll have more time to spend on my social life from now on. Take the next turning on the right. We're nearly there. Look. Only seven more miles.' She pointed at a signpost. 'So you'd better tell me a bit about you.'

Dante slowed the car down as he turned into a narrow lane and thought how differently he might have answered this question a few years back. The first thing he would have said was that he was a twin, because being a twin had felt like a fundamental part of his existence—like they were two parts of the same person. But not any more. He and Dario hadn't spoken in years.

Six years, to be precise—after an episode when anger and resentment had exploded into misunderstanding and turned into a cold and unforgiving rift. He'd discovered that it was easier to act like his brother no longer existed, rather than acknowledge the fact that they no longer communicated. And that it hurt. It hurt like hell.

'But surely you must have looked me up on the internet,' he murmured.

She quickly turned her head to look at him, and for the first time, she seemed uncertain. 'Well, yes. I did.'

'And didn't that tell you everything you wanted to know?'

'Not really. Bits of it were very vague.'

'I pay people a lot of money to keep my profile vague.'

'Why?'

'To avoid the kind of questions you seem intent on asking.'

'It's just down that long drive. The entrance is just past that big tree on the right.' She leaned forward to point her finger, before settling back against the leather car seat. 'It said you had lots of siblings, and there was something about you having a twin brother and I was wondering what it was like to have a twin. If the two of you are psychic, like people say twins can be. And...'

'And what?' he shot out as her words trailed off.

She shrugged. 'There wasn't much information about your parents,' she said quietly.

Dante's fingers tightened around the steering wheel as he drew up outside a huge old house, whose beauty was slightly diminished by shabby paintwork and a general sense of tiredness. Bad enough that Willow Hamilton should have made breezy assumptions about his estranged twin, but worse that she had touched on the one fact which had ruthlessly been eliminated from his history. Didn't she realise that there was a good reason why there was scant mention of his parents in his personal profile?

He felt a slow anger begin to build inside him,

and if it hadn't been for the damned tiara, he would have dropped her off there and then, and driven away so fast that you wouldn't have seen him for smoke. Because personal questions about his family were forbidden; it was one of the ground rules he laid down at the beginning of any date.

But this wasn't a normal date, was it? It was a means to an end. He stared down at her bare knees and felt a whisper of desire. And perhaps it was time he started taking advantage of some of the very obvious compensations available to drive these unwanted irritations from his head.

'I doubt whether knowing about my parentage or siblings is going to be particularly relevant in the circumstances,' he said coolly. 'Of far greater importance is finding out what turns each other on. Because, as lovers, we need to send out the vibe that we've had more than a little…*intimacy*. And in order to convey that to some degree of satisfaction, then I really need to explore you a little more, Willow.'

And before Willow could properly appreciate what was happening, he had undone their seat belts and was pulling her into his arms, as if it was something he had done countless times before. His cold blue eyes swept over her like a searchlight but there was something in their depths which disturbed her. Something which sent foreboding whispering over her spine. Was it the realisation that this man was way too complicated for her to handle and she shouldn't even try? Instinctively, she tried to pull away but he was having none of it, because he gave a silky laugh as he lowered his head to kiss her.

Willow sucked in a disbelieving breath as their lips met, because this wasn't like that lazy kiss at the airport. This was a completely different animal—an unashamed display of potent sensuality. This was Dante Di Sione being outrageously macho and showing her exactly who was in charge. It was a stamp and an unmistakable sexual boast and something told Willow that this emotionless kiss meant nothing to him.

But that didn't stop from her reacting, did it?

It didn't stop her from feeling as if she'd just stepped from the darkest shadows into the brightest sunlight.

His seeking lips coaxed her own apart and she felt the tips of her breasts harden as he deepened the kiss with his tongue. Did he know she was helpless to resist from the moment he'd first touched her? Was that why he splayed his fingers over her dress and began to caress her aching breast? She gave a whimper of pleasure as she lifted her arms to curl them around his neck and felt a rush of heat between her legs—a honeyed throb of need which drove every other thought and feeling straight from her body. It felt so good. Unimaginably good. She felt exultant. Hungry for more. Hungry for him.

Softly, Willow moaned with pleasure and he drew his head away, his blue eyes smoky with desire and an unmistakeable trace of mockery glinting in their lapis lazuli depths.

'Do you want me to stop, Willow?' he taunted softly, his words a delicious caress which whispered over her skin, making her want him to talk to her that way all day long. 'Or do you want me to touch you a little more?'

His hand was now moving beneath the hem of her dress and she held her breath. She could feel the tiptoeing of his fingertips against the bare skin and the heat between her legs was increasing as he started to kiss her again. His words were muffled against her mouth as he repeated that same sensual, taunting question—and all the while he was inching his fingers further and further up her thigh.

'Do you?'

Her heart pounded as she opened her mouth to reply when the sound of footsteps crunching over gravel broke into the kiss like a rock smashing through a thin sheet of ice. Reluctantly Willow opened her eyes and pulled away from him, in time to see her sister's astonished face looking at them through the car window.

CHAPTER FOUR

'FLORA!' SOMEHOW WILLOW managed to stumble her sister's name out through lips which were swollen by the pressure of Dante's kiss. She tried to pull away from him but he wasn't having any of it—keeping his arm anchored tightly around her shoulders. Her voice trembled a little as his fingertips started stroking at the base of her neck, as if he couldn't bear not to be touching her. 'What…what are you doing here?'

But Flora wasn't looking at her. She was staring at Dante as if she couldn't quite believe her eyes. Willow watched as her sister surreptitiously touched her blond hair as if to check that it was pristine—which naturally, it was—and then spread her fingers out over her breastbone, as if to emphasise that at least one of the Hamilton sisters had breasts.

'And just who is *this*, Willow?' she said in a voice which didn't quite manage to hide her disbelief. 'You really must introduce me.'

'He's...' Willow's voice faltered. *He's the man I've bribed to be here. The man who made me feel I was almost going to explode with pleasure, and that was only from a single kiss.*

'My name is Dante Di Sione and I'm Willow's guest for the wedding,' interjected Dante, and Willow saw Flora almost melt as his sensual lips curved into a lazy smile. 'Didn't she tell you I was coming?'

'No,' said Flora crisply. 'No, she did not. We weren't...well, we weren't expecting her to bring anyone—and as a consequence we've made no special allowances. Which means you'll be in Willow's old bedroom, I'm afraid.'

'And is there a problem with Willow's old bedroom?' he questioned.

'I would say there is, especially for a man of

your dimensions.' Flora looked Dante up and down, as if shamelessly assessing his height. 'There's only a single bed.'

Willow wanted to curl up and die, and that was before Dante moved his hand from her neck to place it proprietarily over her thigh. He smiled up at her sister as he pressed his fingers into her flesh. 'Great,' he murmured. 'I do love a good squeeze.'

This clearly wasn't the reaction Flora had expected and the sight of Dante with his hand on her sister's leg must have confused the life out of her. But a lifetime of social training meant that her irritation didn't last long and she made an instant recovery. 'If you'd like to park over by the stables, Dante.' She flashed him a glossy smile. 'Once you've settled in we'll be serving coffee in the drawing room and you'll be able to meet my mother. Oh, and you'll have to try on your bridesmaid dress again, Willow—though I warn you that Clover is going to go ballistic if you've lost any more weight! And don't you think you ought to put a cardigan on? Your arms are covered in goose bumps.'

Dante started up the engine as they watched Flora walk into the main entrance of the grand house. Her blond hair swung down her back in a glossy curtain and she walked with the confident wiggle of a beautiful woman who knew she was being watched.

'So that's one of your sisters,' he said slowly as she disappeared through the open front door.

'Yes.' Willow nodded her head. *So get in first*, she thought. *Say all the stuff he must be thinking and that way you won't come over as vulnerable.* 'I told you my siblings were gorgeous, didn't I? And Flora especially so. Every man she meets falls in love with her. I...I think maybe she's single at the moment, though you can never be...'

'Willow.' He halted her flow of words by placing his finger firmly over her lips. 'Will you please shut up? I may have something of a reputation where women are concerned but even I would draw the line at going to a wedding with one sister, and then making out with another.'

'Not taking into account the fact that she might not be interested in you,' she said indignantly.

'No, of course not,' he murmured as he started up the engine. 'She was looking at me with nothing but cool indifference in her eyes.'

Willow couldn't decide whether to pull him up for his arrogance or simply acknowledge that he was telling the truth, because Flora *had* been looking at him as if she'd like to eat him up for breakfast, lunch and dinner and then maybe go back for a midnight snack. And yet he had been kissing *her*, hadn't he? Kissing her in a way she'd never been kissed before. She could still recall the fizzing excitement in her blood and the way she'd wanted to dissolve beneath his seeking fingers. She'd wanted him to carry on burrowing his fingers beneath her dress and to touch her where she was all hot and aching. Would he laugh or be horrified if he knew she'd never felt like that before? Would he be horrified to discover that she'd never actually had sex before?

They parked the car and she led Dante through the house by one of the back doors, beginning to realise what a big gamble she'd taken by bringing him here. Was he really a good enough actor to pretend to be interested in her when there was going to be so much Grade One crumpet sashaying around the place in their killer heels?

She pushed open the door of her old bedroom, the room where she had spent so much of her childhood—and immediately it felt like stepping back in time. It always did. It made her feel weird and it made her feel small. Little had changed since she'd left home, and whenever she came here, it felt as if her past had been preserved in aspic—and for the first time, she began to question why. Had her parents' refusal to redecorate been based on a longstanding wish not to tempt fate by changing things around?

Willow looked around. There was the portrait done of her when she was six—years before the illness had taken hold—with a blue sparkly clip in her blond hair. How innocent she looked. How totally oblivious to what lay ahead. Next to it was the first embroidery she'd ever done—a sweet, framed cross-stitch saying *Home Sweet Home*. And there were her books—row upon row of them—her beloved connection to the outside world and her only real escape from the sickroom, apart from her sewing. Later on, she'd discovered films—and the more slushy and happy-ever-after, the better. Because fantasy had been a whole lot better than reality.

Sometimes it had felt as if she'd been living in a gilded cage, even though she knew there had been good reasons for that—mainly to keep her away from any rogue infections. But her inevitable isolation and the corresponding protectiveness of her family had left her ill-equipped to deal with certain situations. Like now. She'd missed out on so much. Even at college she'd been watched over and protected by Flora and Clover, who had both been studying at the same university. For a long time she'd only had the energy to deal with maintaining her health and completing her studies and getting a decent degree—she hadn't had the confidence to add men into the mix, even if she'd found anyone attractive enough.

And she had never found anyone as attractive as Dante Di Sione.

She watched him put their bags down and walk over to the window to stare out at the wide green-grey sweep of the Sussex Downs, before turning to face her—his incredible lapis lazuli eyes narrowed. She waited for him to make some comment about the view, or to remark on the massive dimensions of her rather crumbling but beautiful old home, but to her surprise he did neither.

'So,' he said, beginning to walk towards her with stealthy grace. 'How long have we got?'

'Got?' she repeated blankly, not quite sure of his meaning even when he pulled her into his arms and started trailing his fingertips over her body so that she began to shiver beneath the filmy fabric of her delicate dress. 'For…for what?'

Dante smiled, but it was a smile edged with impatience and a danger that even Willow could recognise was sexual.

'That depends on you, and what you want.'

'What I want?' she said faintly.

'Forgive me if I'm mistaken, but I thought that you were as frustrated by your sister's interruption as I was. I was under the distinct impression that our fake relationship was about to get real, and in a very satisfying way. It would certainly be more convincing if we were properly intimate instead of just pretending to be. So are we going to play games with each other or are we going to give in to what we both clearly want?' he murmured as he began to stroke her breasts. 'And have sex?'

Willow quivered as her nipples tightened beneath his expert touch and even though his words were completely unromantic…even though they were the direct opposite of all those mushy romcoms she used to watch—they were still making her *feel* something, weren't they? They were making her feel like a woman. A *real* woman—not some pale and bloodless creature who'd spent so much time being hooked up to an intravenous drip, while cocktails of drugs were pumped into her system.

Yet this hadn't been what she'd planned when she'd rashly demanded he accompany her here. She'd thought they were engaging in nothing more than an indifferent barter of things they both wanted. Unless she wasn't being honest with herself. *Face the truth, Willow.* And wasn't the truth that from the moment she'd seen him walk into the Caribbean airport terminal, her body had sprung into life with a feeling of lust like she'd never felt before? In which case—why was she hesitating? Wasn't this whole trip supposed to be about changing her life around? To start living like other women her age did.

She tipped up her face so that he could kiss her

again. 'Have sex,' she said boldly, meeting the flicker of humour in his smoky blue gaze.

He smiled and then suddenly what was happening *did* feel like a fantasy. Like every one of those mushy films she'd watched. He picked her up and carried her across the room, placing her down on the bed and pausing only to remove the battered old teddy bear that used to accompany her everywhere. She felt a wave of embarrassment as he pushed the bear onto the floor, but then he was bending his lips to hers and suddenly he was kissing her.

It was everything a kiss ought to be. Passionate. Searching. Deep. It made Willow squirm restlessly beneath him, her fingers beginning to scrabble at his shirt as she felt the rush of molten heat between her legs. And maybe he had guessed what was happening—or maybe this was just the way he operated—but he slid his hand beneath her skirt and all the way up her leg, pushing aside the damp panel of her knickers and beginning to tease her there with his finger. Her eyes fluttered to a close and it felt so *perfect* that Willow wanted to cry out her pleasure—but maybe he anticipated that too, because he deepened the kiss. And suddenly it became different. It became hard and hungry and demanding and she was matching it with her own demands—arching her body up towards his, as if she couldn't get close enough.

She could feel the hardness at his groin—the unfamiliar rocky ridge nudging insistently against her—and to her surprise she wasn't daunted, or scared. Maybe it was just her poor starved body demanding what nature had intended it for, because suddenly she was writhing against him—moaning her eagerness and her impatience into his open mouth.

He reached for his belt and Willow heard the rasp of his zip as he began to lower it, when suddenly there was a loud knock on the door.

They both froze and Willow shrank back against the pillows, trying to get her ragged breath back, though it took several seconds before she could speak.

'Who is it?' she demanded in a strangled voice.

'Willow?'

Willow's heart sank. It was Clover's voice. Clover, the bride-to-be. Well-meaning and bossy Clover, the older sister who had protected her as fiercely as a lioness would protect one of her cubs. Just like the rest of her family.

'H-hi, Clover,' she said shakily.

'Can I come in?

Before Willow could answer, Dante shook his head and mouthed, *No*, but she knew what would happen if she didn't comply. There would be an outraged family discussion downstairs. There would be talk of rudeness. They would view Dante with even more suspicion than she suspected he was already going to encounter. The atmosphere would be spoiled before the wedding celebrations had even begun.

She shook her head as she tugged her dress back down, her cheeks flaming bright red as she readjusted her knickers. 'Hang on a minute,' she called, wriggling out of Dante's arms and off the bed, mouthing, *Don't say a word.*

His responding look indicated that he didn't really have much choice but there was no disguising the flicker of fury sparking in his blue eyes.

Willow scuttled over to the door and pulled it open by a crack to see Clover outside, her hair in rollers and an expression on her face which couldn't seem to make up its mind whether to be cross or curious.

'What the hell are you doing?' Clover asked sharply.

For a minute Willow was tempted to tell her to mind her own business, or at least to use her imagination. To snap back that she had just been enjoying a glorious initiation to the mysteries of sex when she had been so rudely interrupted. What was it with her sisters that they kept bursting in on her at the most inopportune moments? But then she reminded herself of everything that Clover had done for her. All those nights she'd sat beside her, holding her hand and helping her keep the nightmares at bay.

Telling herself that her sister was only acting with the best intentions, Willow gave a helpless kind of smile. 'I was just showing Dante the amazing view of the Sussex Downs.'

Clover slanted her a *who-do-you-think-you're-kidding?* look. 'Ah, yes,' she said, loud enough for the entire first floor corridor to hear. 'Dante. The mystery man who drove you here.'

'My guest,' said Willow indignantly.

'Why didn't you tell us you were bringing him?' said Clover.

'Maybe she wanted it to be a surprise,' came a drawling voice, and Willow didn't need to turn round to know that Dante had walked up behind her. She could tell from her sister's goggle-eyed expression even before he placed his hand on her shoulder and started massaging it, the way she'd seen people do in films when they were trying to help their partner relax. *So why did the tight tension inside her body suddenly feel as if it was spiralling out of control?*

'This is…this is Dante,' she said, hearing the hesitance of her words. 'Dante Di Sione.'

'I'm very pleased to meet you, Dante.' Clover's face took on the judgemental expression for which she was famous within the family. 'Perhaps Willow could bear to share you enough to bring you downstairs for coffee, so that everyone can meet you. My mother is particularly keen to make your acquaintance.'

'I can hardly wait,' murmured Dante, increasing the pressure of his impromptu massage by a fraction.

Willow had barely shut the door on her sister before Dante turned her round to face him, his hands on her upper arms, his lapis lazuli gaze boring into her.

'Why do you let her speak to you like that?' he demanded. 'Why didn't you just ignore her, or tell her you were busy? Surely she has enough imagination to realise we were making out?'

Willow gave a half-hearted shrug. 'She's very persistent. They all are.'

He frowned. 'What usually happens when you bring a man home with you?'

Willow licked her lips. Now they were on dangerous territory, and if she told him the truth, she suspected he'd run a mile. Instead, she shot him a challenging look. 'Why, are you afraid of my sisters, Dante?'

'I don't give a damn about your sisters.' He pulled her close against him. 'I'd just like to continue what we were doing a few minutes ago. Now...' His hand cupped her aching breast once more. 'Where were we, can you remember?'

For a minute Willow let him caress her nipple and her eyes fluttered to a close as he began to nuzzle at her neck. She could feel the renewed rush of heat to her body and she wondered how long it would take. Whether they would have time to do it properly. But what if it hurt? What if she *bled*? Pulling away from him, she met the frustration in his eyes.

Was she about to lose her mind? *Of course they wouldn't have time.* She'd waited a long time to have sex—years and years, to be precise—so why rush it and then have to go downstairs in an embarrassing walk of shame, to face her judgemental family who would be assembled in the drawing room like a circle of vultures?

'We've got to go downstairs,' she said. 'For… for coffee.'

'I don't want coffee,' he growled. 'I want you.'

There was a pause before she could summon up the courage to say it and when she did it came out in a breathless rush. 'And I want you.'

'So?'

'So I'm going to be a bridesmaid and I have to get my hair and make-up done before the ceremony.' She swallowed. 'And there'll be plenty of time for that…later.'

Knowing he was fighting a losing battle—something he always went out of his way to avoid—Dante walked over to the window, trying to calm his acutely aroused body before having to go downstairs to face her frightful family.

He wondered what had made her so surprisingly compliant when her sister had come up here snooping around. He wondered what had happened to the woman who had flirted so boldly with him at the airport. The one who had demanded he be her escort as the price for returning his bag. He'd had her down as one of those independent free spirits who would give great sex—and her going-up-in-flames reaction every time he laid a finger on her had only reinforced that theory.

Yet from the moment he'd driven up the long drive to her impressive but rather faded country house, she had become ridiculously docile. He stared out at the breathtaking view. The magnificence of the distant landscape reminded him of his own family home, back in the States. Somewhere he'd left when he'd gone away to boarding school at the age of eight, and to which he had never really returned. Certainly not for any great length of time. His mouth twisted. Because wasn't it something of a travesty to call the Long Island place a *family home*? It was nothing but a grand house built on some very expensive real estate—with a magnificent facade which concealed all kinds of dirty secrets.

He turned back to find Willow watching him, her grey gaze wary and her manner slightly hesitant—as if she expected him to say that he had changed his mind and was about to leave. He suddenly found himself thinking that she reminded him of a delicate gazelle.

'Why are you suddenly so uptight?' he questioned. 'Is something wrong?'

Willow stilled and if she hadn't fancied him so much she might have told him the whole story. But it was precisely *because* she fancied him so much that she couldn't. He'd start treating her differently. He'd be overcautious when he touched her. He might not even *want* to touch her. Because that was the thing with illness—it did more than affect the person it struck; it affected everyone around you. People who were mature and sensible might try to deny it, but didn't they sometimes behave as if the illness she'd once had was in some way contagious?

And why *shouldn't* she forget about that period in her life? She'd been given the all-clear ages ago and now was her chance to get something she'd wanted for a very long time. Something as powerful and as uncomplicated as sexual fulfilment, with a man she suspected would be perfect for the purpose, as long as she reminded herself not to read too much into it. For the first time in her life, she had to reach out for what she wanted. Not the things that other women wanted—because she wasn't asking for the impossible. She wasn't clamouring for marriage and babies—just a brief and heady sexual relationship with Dante Di Sione. But she had to be proactive.

She smiled into his hard blue eyes. 'I think it's because I'm the youngest, and they've always been a little protective of me. You know how it is.' She began to walk across the room towards him, plucking up the courage to put her arms around his neck. This close she could see into his eyes perfectly. And although she was short on experience, she recognised the desire which was making them grow so smoky.

And if she detected a flicker of suspicion lurking in their depths, then surely it was up to her to keep those suspicions at bay.

'I don't want to do it in a rush. I want to savour every single moment,' she whispered, trying to sound as if she made sexual assignations with men every day of the week. 'And don't they say that the best things in life are worth waiting for?'

He framed her face in his hands and there was a split second when she thought he was about to bend his head and kiss her, but he didn't. He just stared at her for a very long time, with the kind of look in his eyes which made a shiver trickle down her spine.

'I hear what you're saying and I am prepared to take it on board. But be very clear that I am not a patient man, Willow—and I have a very low boredom threshold. Better not keep me waiting too long,' he said roughly as he levered her away from him, in the direction of the door.

CHAPTER FIVE

DANTE GLANCED AROUND at the guests who were standing on the newly mown lawn drinking champagne. He risked another glance at his watch and wondered how soon this would be over and he could get Willow into bed—but like all weddings, this one seemed never-ending.

The place had been a hive of activity all afternoon. The faded grandeur of Willow's vast home had been transformed by legions of adoring locals, who had carried armfuls of flowers from the nearby village to decorate the house and gardens. Hedges had been trimmed and Chinese lanterns strung high in the trees. Rough wooden trestle tables had been covered with white cloths before being decked with grapes and roses and tiny flickering tealights.

It quickly dawned on him that the Hamiltons were the kind of aristocratic family with plenty of cachet but very little cash. The ceremony had taken place in *their own church*—he found that quite hard to believe—a small but freezing building situated within the extensive grounds. The bride looked okay—but then, all brides looked the same, in Dante's opinion. She wore a white dress and a veil and the service had been interminable. No change there. But he'd found himself unable to tear his eyes away from Willow as she'd made her way up the aisle. He thought how beautiful she looked, despite a deeply unflattering dress and a smile which suggested that, like him, she'd rather be somewhere else.

Before the ceremony he had endured a meet-and-greet with her family over some unspeakable coffee, drunk in a room hung with dusty old paintings. Flora and Clover he'd already met and the remaining sibling was called Poppy—a startlingly pretty girl with grey eyes like Willow's, who seemed as keen to question him as her sisters had been. Their attitude towards him had been one of unrestrained suspicion. They were curious about where he and Willow had met and how long they'd been an item. They seemed surprised to hear he lived in Paris and they wondered how often he was seeing their sister. And because Dante didn't like being interrogated and because he wasn't sure what Willow had told them, he was deliberately vague.

Her parents had appeared at one point. Her mother was tall and still beautiful, with cheekbones as high as Willow's own. She was wearing what looked like her husband's old smoking jacket over a dress and a pair of wellington boots and smiled rather distractedly when Dante shook her hand.

But her attitude changed the instant she caught sight of Willow, who had been over on the other side of the room, finding him a cup of coffee. 'Are you okay, darling? You're not tiring yourself out?'

Just what *was* it with these people? Dante wondered. Was that a warning look from Sister Number Three being slanted in his direction? He *got* that Willow probably didn't bring a lot of men home and he *got* that as the youngest daughter she would be a little overprotected. But they seemed to be fussing around her as if she was some kind of teenager, rather than a woman in her mid-twenties. And she seemed to be letting them.

But now the wedding was over, the photo session was finished and he was standing on a warm summer's evening with a growing sense of sexual anticipation. He felt his mouth dry as he glanced across the lawn, to where Willow was listening to something her mother was saying, obediently nodding her blond head, which was woven with blooms and making her look even more ethereal than before. Her dress emphasised the razor-sharp slant of her collarbones and the slenderness of her bare arms.

Maybe her intrinsic delicacy was the reason why everyone seemed to treat her with kid gloves. And why her gaggle of interfering sisters seemed to boss her around so much.

Her mother walked off and Dante put his untouched drink onto a table, walking through the growing dusk until he was standing in front of her. He watched as her expression underwent a series of changes. He saw shyness as well as that now-familiar wariness in her eyes, but he saw desire too—and that desire lit something inside him and made him want to touch her again.

'Dance with me,' he said.

With a quick bite of her lip, she shook her head. 'I'd better not. I have masses of things I need to do.'

'It wasn't a question, Willow,' he said, pulling her into his arms. 'It was a command and I won't tolerate anyone who disobeys my commands.'

'That's an outrageous thing to say.'

'So outrageous it's made you shiver with desire?'

'I'm not.'

'Yes, you are.' Pulling her against his body,

he breathed in the scent of flowers which made him long to remove that fussy dress and have her naked in his arms. He'd had enough of behaving like a teenager—only getting so far before another of her damned sisters interrupted them. He slid his hand over her ribcage, his heart thundering as his fingertips stroked the slippery satin. 'So how long does this damned wedding go on for?'

'Oh, ages,' she said, but the sudden breathlessness in her voice coincided with his thumb casually beginning to circle the area beneath her breast. 'We haven't even had the speeches yet.'

'That's what's worrying me,' he said, swinging her round and thinking how slight she was. He remembered how feather-light she'd felt when he'd carried her over to that ridiculously tiny bed and he wished he was on that bed right now with his mouth on her breast and his fingers between her legs. 'I don't know how much longer I can wait,' he said huskily.

'Wait?' She drew her head back and it was as

if she had suddenly recognised her power over him, because her grey eyes were dancing with mischief. 'Yes, I suppose you must be hungry. Well, don't worry—supper won't be long. Just as soon as my father and the best man have spoken.'

In answer, he pressed his hardness against her with a sudden calculated stamp of sexual mastery and watched as her pupils dilated in response. 'I want you,' he said, very deliberately. 'And I'm tempted to take you by the hand and get us lost in these enormous grounds. I'd like to find some-where sheltered, like the shade of a big tree, so that I could explore what you're wearing under-neath that monstrosity of a dress. I'd like to make you come very quickly. In fact, I think I could make myself come right now, just by thinking about it.'

'Dante!'

'Yes, Willow?'

She drew away from him, trembling slightly, and once again he was confused, because wasn't she just a mass of contradictions? One minute she was so hot that he almost scorched his fingers when he touched her—and the next she was looking up at him with reproachful grey eyes, like some delicate flower he was in danger of crushing beneath the full force of his desire. And that was how her family treated her, wasn't it? Like she couldn't be trusted to make her own judgements and look after herself.

'You're very…'

'Very what?' He stalled her sentence with the brush of his lips against her cheek and felt her shiver again.

'D-demanding,' she managed.

'Don't you like me being demanding?'

Willow closed her eyes as he tightened his arms around her, distracted by the heat of his body and acutely aware that they were being watched. *Of course they were being watched.* Dante Di Sione was easily the most watchable man here—and hadn't that been one of the reasons she'd demanded his company? To show people that she was capable of attracting such a man? But suddenly it felt like much more than just *pretending* to be his lover; she wanted to *be* his lover. She wanted it to be real. She wanted to be like everyone else, but she couldn't. So she was just going to have to make the best of what she was capable of, wasn't she?

'Yes,' she whispered. 'I like it very much. It's just not very appropriate right now. We're in the middle of a crowd of people and there are things I'm supposed to be doing.'

'Like what?'

'Checking that everyone's got a drink so they can make a toast once the speeches start. And introducing people who don't know each other— that sort of thing.'

'All this hanging around and waiting is very dull,' he observed.

'Then circulate,' she said lightly. 'That's what people do.'

'I've done nothing *but* circulate,' he growled. 'I think I'll go crazy if I have to endure yet another society matron trying to calculate what my net worth is.'

She tilted her head back and studied him. 'So how do you usually cope with weddings?'

'By avoiding them whenever possible.'

'But you were unable to avoid this one?'

'It seems I was.'

She narrowed her eyes at him. 'There must be something very valuable in that bag to make you want it so much.'

'Right now, I want you far more than anything in that damned bag.'

Willow giggled, feeling a sudden heady rush of excitement which had more to do with the way he was making her feel than the glass of punch she'd drunk. 'Which was a very neat way of avoiding my question.'

'I don't remember you actually asking a question and it's the only answer you're going to get. So when can we leave?'

'After the cake has been cut,' she said breathlessly. 'Look, there are the main players getting ready to speak and I'm supposed to be up at the top table. I'll see you in a while.'

She tore herself away from his arms, aware of his gaze burning into her as she walked across the garden, but at that moment she was on such a high that she felt as if she could have floated over the candlelit lawn.

It didn't take Flora long to bring her right back down to earth as she joined her in the throng of Hamiltons at the top table.

'I've looked him up on the internet,' she said as soon as Willow was in earshot.

'Who?'

'Who do you think? The man who drove you here today in his flashy red sports car,' replied her sister. 'Mr Macho.'

Willow reached for a glass of champagne from a passing waitress and took a sip as her gaze drifted over towards Dante's statuesque form, which seemed to stand out from the milling crowd. 'He's gorgeous, isn't he?' she said, without really thinking.

'Nobody's denying that,' said Flora slowly. 'And I'm guessing that if you've brought him here, it must be serious?'

'Well, I suppose so,' said Willow evasively.

Flora lowered her voice. 'So you're aware that he's an *international playboy* with lovers in every major city in the world who is also known as a complete maverick in the world of business?'

Willow took a mouthful of fizz. 'So what? I'm not planning some kind of corporate takeover with him.'

'He's way out of your league, love,' said Flora gently. 'He's a wolf and you're an innocent little lamb. You haven't exactly had a lot of experience with the opposite sex, have you?'

'Only because my family is too busy mounting an armed guard around me!'

Flora frowned. 'So what exactly is going on between you?'

There was a pause. 'I like him,' said Willow truthfully. 'I like him a lot.'

It was perhaps unfortunate that Great-aunt

Maud should have chosen just that moment to drift past in a cloud of magenta chiffon and gardenia perfume, blinking rapidly as she caught the tail end of their conversation. 'So does that mean you're going to be next up the aisle, Willow?' She beamed, without waiting for an answer. 'I must say I'm not surprised. He is quite something, that young man of yours. Quite something.'

Dante listened to the formal speeches which always bored the hell out of him and steadfastly ignored the redhead who was flashing him an eager smile. But for once the sentiments expressed went beyond the usual gags about mothers-in-law and shotguns. The groom thanked all the bridesmaids and told them how beautiful they looked, but he left Willow until last, and suddenly his voice grew serious.

'I'd just like to say how much it meant to Clover, having Willow's support. But much more than that is having her here today, looking so lovely. It means…well, it means everything to us.'

Dante frowned as people began to cheer, wondering why the atmosphere had grown distinctly *poignant* and why Willow's mother was suddenly groping in her bag for a handkerchief.

But then Willow's father began speaking and after he had waxed long and lyrical about the bride, he paused before resuming—his eyes resting affectionately on the slender blonde in the bridesmaid dress who was twisting the peachy satin around her fingers and looking slightly awkward.

'I just want to echo Dominic's words and say how happy we are to see Willow here today looking, if I might add, positively radiant. We just want her to know how proud we are of her, and the way she handled her illness, when all her peers were running around without a care in the world. And how her recovery has made us all feel very, very grateful.'

The applause which followed was deafening

and Dante's lips froze as suddenly it all made sense.

Of *course.*

That's why she looked so fragile and that's why her family fussed around her and were so protective of her.

She'd been ill.

How ill? It must have been bad for it to warrant a mention in not one but *two* of the wedding speeches.

He felt momentarily winded. Like that time when a tennis ball hit by his twin had slammed straight into his solar plexus. He had been itching to take Willow away from here as soon as the speeches were over, but suddenly he needed time. And distance. Because how could he now take her to bed in the light of what he had learned?

Did Willow sense where he was in the throng of people? Was that why her grey eyes suddenly turned to meet his? Only this time it was more than desire which pumped through his veins as his gaze connected with hers. It was a cocktail of emotions he was unfamiliar with. He felt sympathy and a flare of something which clenched his heart with a sensation close to pain. The sense that life was unfair. And yet why should that come as a surprise, when he'd learnt the lesson of life's unfairness at the age of eight, when his entire world had changed for ever?

Why the hell hadn't she told him?

He watched as the smile she was directing at him became slightly uncertain and she picked up her glass and took a mouthful of champagne. And part of him wanted to run. To get into his car and drive back to London. To fly on to Paris as soon as possible and put this whole incident behind him. Yet he couldn't do that—and not just because she still had his grandfather's precious tiara. He couldn't just turn his back on her and walk away. If she'd known real suffering, then she deserved his compassion and his respect.

He saw all the women lining up and giggling and wondered what was happening, when he realised that the bride was about to throw her bouquet. And he wondered why it came as no real sense of surprise when Willow caught it, to the accompaniment of more loud cheers.

He couldn't stay here. He could see some of her relatives smiling at him, almost—*God forbid*— as if they were preparing to welcome him into the fold and he knew that he had to act. Ignoring the redhead with the cleavage who had been edging closer and closer, he walked straight up to Willow and took the empty champagne glass from her hand.

'Let's get out of here.'

He couldn't miss the look of relief on her face.

'I thought you'd never ask,' she said, sounding a little unsteady.

On her high-heeled shoes she was tottering as they walked across the darkening grass as if she'd had a little too much to drink—but for once Dante wasn't about to take the moral high ground.

He waited for her to mention the speeches, but she didn't. She was too busy weaving her fingers into his and squeezing them. He thought again about her father's words and how her experience had affected her. It meant she'd probably learnt in the hardest way possible about the fragility of life and the random way that trouble could strike. He wondered if she'd plumped for recklessness as a result of that. Was that why she would have had sex with him before the wedding had even started, if her damned sister hadn't interrupted them? He wondered if she was this free with everyone—an aristocratic wild child who'd learned to be liberal with her body. And he was unprepared for the sudden dark shaft of anger which slammed into him.

They reached her room without meeting anyone and the sounds of celebration drifted up through the open windows as she shut the bedroom door behind them and switched on a small lamp. He could hear music and laughter and the rising lull of snatched conversation, but there was no joy in Dante's heart right then.

She leaned against the door, her shiny ruffled dress gleaming and her grey eyes looking very bright. 'So,' she said, darting a rather embarrassed glance at the bride's bouquet she was still holding, before quickly putting it down on a nearby table. 'Now what?'

He wished he could wipe what he'd heard from his mind, leaving his conscience free to do what he really wanted—which was to walk over there and remove her dress. To take off her bra and her panties and strip himself bare, before entering that pale and slim body with one slow and exquisite thrust.

He went to stand by the window, with his back to the strings of Chinese lanterns which gleamed in the trees.

'Did you enjoy the wedding, Willow?' he asked carefully.

She walked across the room, pulling the wilting crown of flowers from her head and placing it on the dressing table, and a clip which clattered onto the wooden floor sounded unnaturally loud.

'It was okay,' she said, taking out another clip,

and then another, before putting them down. She turned around then, her hair spilling over her shoulders, and there was a faint look of anxiety in her eyes, as if she had just picked up from his tone that something was different. She licked her lips. 'Did you?'

He shook his head. 'No, not really. But then, I'm not really a big fan of weddings.'

Her smile became a little brittle. 'Oh, well, at least it's over now,' she said. 'So why don't we just take our minds off it?'

She began to walk unsteadily towards him and Dante knew he had to stop this before it went any further. Before he did something he might later regret. But it was hard to resist her when she looked so damned lovely. There was something so compelling about her. Something pure and untouched which contrasted with the hungry look in her eyes and the wanton spill of her half-pinned hair. She looked like a little girl playing the part of vamp.

He shook his head. 'No, Willow.'

But she kept on walking towards him until she was standing in front of him in her long dress. And now she was winding her arms around his neck and clinging on to him like a tender vine and the desire to kiss her was like a fever raging in his blood.

Briefly, he closed his eyes as if that would help him resist temptation, but it didn't—because the feel of her was just as distracting as the sight of her. And maybe she took that as an invitation— because she brushed her mouth over his with a tentative exploration which made him shiver. With an angry little groan he succumbed to the spiralling of desire as he deepened the kiss. He felt the kick of his heart as her hands began to move rather frantically over him, and what could he do but respond?

She was tugging at his tie as he started to caress the slender lines of her body, his fingers sliding helplessly over the slippery material. He felt her sway and picked her up, carrying her over to the bed, like a man acting on autopilot. She lay there, almost swamped by the silky folds of her bridesmaid dress, and as his hand reached out to stroke its way over her satin-covered breast, he felt a savage jerk of lust.

'Oh, Dante,' she breathed—and that heartfelt little note of wonder was almost his undoing.

Would it be so wrong to take her? To have her gasp out her pleasure and him do the same, especially when they both wanted it so badly? Surely it would be a *good* thing to end this rather bizarre day with some uncomplicated and mindless sex.

Except that it wouldn't be uncomplicated. Or mindless. Not in the light of what he'd learned. Because she was vulnerable. Of course she was. And he couldn't treat her as he would treat any other woman. He couldn't just strip her naked and pleasure her and take what he wanted for himself before walking away. She had gone through too much to be treated as something disposable.

With an effort which tore at him like a physical pain, he moved away from the bed and went to stand by the window, where the darkness of the garden was broken by the flickering gleam of candlelight. Tiny pinpricks of light glittered on every surface, like fallen stars. Beneath the open window he could hear a couple talking in low voices which then abruptly stopped and some- thing told him they were kissing. Was that envy he felt? Envy that he couldn't just forget every- thing he knew and block out his reservations with a kiss?

It took several moments for the hunger to leave him, and when he had composed himself suf- ficiently, he turned back to find her sitting up on the bed looking at him—confusion alternat- ing with the desire which was skating across her fine-boned features.

He drew in a deep breath. 'Why didn't you tell me you'd been so ill?'

Willow's first reaction was one of rage as his words fired into her skin like sharp little ar- rows. Rage that her father and Dominic should have seen fit to include the information *in their speeches* and rage that he should suddenly have started talking to her in that new and gentle voice. She didn't want him to be *gentle* with her—she wanted him hot and hungry. She wanted him tugging impatiently at her clothes like he'd been before, as if he couldn't wait to strip her bare.

'What does that have to do with anything?' she demanded. 'I had leukaemia as a child. What's the big deal?'

'It's a pretty big deal, Willow.'

'Only if people choose to make it one,' she gritted out. 'Especially since I've had the all-clear, which makes me as disease-free as you or the rest of the general population. What did you want me to do, Dante? Tell you all about the drugs and the side effects and the way my hair fell out, or how difficult it was to actually keep food down? When it comes to interacting with men, it's not exactly what they want to hear as a chat-up line. It doesn't really make you attractive towards the opposite sex.' She glared. 'Why the hell did Dom and my father have to say anything?'

'I think I might have worked it out for myself,'

he said slowly. 'Because I'd had my suspicions ever since we arrived.'

'You had your *suspicions*?' she echoed angrily.

'Sure. I wondered why your sisters were acting as if I was the big, bad ogre and I wondered why everyone was so protective of you. It took me a while to work out why that might be, but now I think I have.'

'So once I was very sick and now I'm not,' she said flippantly. 'End of subject, surely?'

'But it's a little bit more complicated than that, Willow?' he said slowly. 'Isn't it?'

For a minute she stiffened as she thought he might have learned about her biggest fear and secret, before she told herself he couldn't know. He wasn't *that* perceptive and she'd certainly never discussed it with anyone else. 'What are you talking about?' she questioned.

His eyes narrowed. 'Something tells me you've never brought a man back here before. Have you?'

Willow felt humiliation wash over her and in

that moment she hated Dante Di Sione's perception and that concerned way he was looking at her. She didn't want him looking at her with *concern*—she wanted him looking at her with *lust. So brazen it out*, she told herself. *You've come this far. You've dismissed your illness, so deal with the rest.* She had him here with her—a captive audience—and judging by his body language, he still wanted her just as much as she wanted him.

'And how did you manage to work that out?' she questioned.

His eyes were boring into her, still with that horrible, unwanted perception.

'Just that every time I was introduced as your partner, people expressed a kind of barely concealed astonishment. I mean, I know I have something of a reputation where women are concerned, but they were acting like I was the devil incarnate.'

For a second Willow thought about lying to him. About telling him that his was just another anonymous face in a sea of men she'd brought here. But why tell him something she'd be unable to carry off? She didn't think she was *that* good a liar. And all she wanted was for that warm feeling to come back. She wanted him to kiss her again. She wasn't asking for commitment—she knew she could never be in a position to ask for that. All she wanted was to be in his arms again.

She thought about the person she'd been when he'd met her at the airport—that bold and flirtatious Willow she'd never dared be before—and Dante had seemed to like that Willow, hadn't he? She was certainly a more attractive proposition than the woman sitting huddled on the bed, meekly listening to him berate her.

'I thought you would be the kind of man who wouldn't particularly want a woman to burden you with every second of her past.'

'That much is true,' he conceded reluctantly.

'So, what's your beef?'

Rather unsteadily, she got off the bed, and before he could stop her she'd reached behind her to slide down the zip of her bridesmaid dress, so that it pooled around her ankles in a shimmering circle.

Willow had never stood in front of a man in her underwear before and she'd always wondered what it would feel like—whether she would feel shy or uninhibited or just plain self-conscious. But she could still feel the effect of the champagne she'd drunk and, more than that, the look on his face was powerful enough to drive every inhibition from her mind. Because Dante looked almost *tortured* as she stepped out from the circle of satin and stood before him wearing nothing but her underwear and a pair of high-heeled shoes.

And although people often told her she looked as if she could do with a decent meal, Willow knew from her time working in the fashion industry that slenderness worked in your favour when you were wearing nothing but a bra and a pair of pants. She could see his gaze lingering on the swell of her breasts in the ivory-coloured lace bra which was embroidered with tiny roses. Reluctantly, it travelled down to her bare stomach before seeming to caress the matching thong, lingering longest on the flimsy triangle and making her ache there.

Feeling as if she was playing out a part she'd seen in a film, she lifted her fingers to her breast and cupped the slight curve. As she ran her finger along a twist of leaves, she thought she saw him move, as if he was about to cross the room and take her in his arms after all, and she held her breath in anticipation.

But he didn't.

Instead a little nerve began working furiously at his temple as he patted his pocket, until he'd found his car keys.

'And I think that's my cue to leave,' he said harshly.

'No!' The word came out in a rush. 'Please, Dante. I don't want you to go.'

'I'm sorry. I'm out of here.'

'Dante…'

'No. Listen to me, Willow.' There was a pause while he seemed to be composing himself, and when he started speaking, his words sounded very controlled. 'For what it's worth, I think you're lovely. Very lovely. A beautiful butterfly of a woman. But I'm not going to have sex with you.'

She swallowed. 'Because you don't want me?'

His voice grew rough. 'You know damned well I want you.'

She lifted her eyes to his. 'Then why?'

He seemed to hesitate and Willow got the distinct feeling that he was going to say something dismissive, or tell her that he didn't owe her any kind of explanation. But to her surprise, he didn't. His expression took on that almost gentle look again and she found herself wanting to hurl something at him…preferably herself. To tell him not to wrap her up in cotton wool the way everyone else did. To treat her like she was made of flesh and blood instead of something fragile and breakable. To make her feel like that passionate woman he'd brought to life in his arms.

'Because I'm the kind of man who brings women pain, and you've probably had enough of that in your life. Don't make yourself the willing recipient of any more.' He met the question in her eyes. 'I'm incapable of giving women what they want and I'm not talking about sex. I don't do emotion, or love, or commitment, because I don't really know how those things work. When people tell me that I'm cold and unfeeling, I don't get offended—because I know it's true. There's nothing deep about me, Willow—and there never will be.'

Willow drew in a breath. It was now or never. It was a huge risk—but so what? What did she have to lose when the alternative of not having him suddenly seemed unbearable? 'But that's all I want from you,' she whispered. 'Sex.'

His face hardened as he shook his head.

'And I certainly don't have sex with virgins,' he finished flatly.

She stared at him in disbelief. 'But…how on earth could you tell I was a virgin?' she whispered, her voice quivering with disappointment, before realising from his brief, hard smile that she had just walked into some sort of trap.

'Call it an informed guess,' he said drily. 'And it's the reason why I have to leave.'

The hurt and the rejection Willow was feeling was now replaced by a far more real concern as she realised he meant it. He was going to leave her there, aching and alone and having to face everyone in the morning.

Reaching down to the bed, she grabbed at the duvet which was lying on the bed and wrapped it around herself, so that it covered her in an unflattering white cloud. And then she looked into the icy glitter of his eyes, willing him not to walk away. 'If you go now, it will just cause a big scene. It will make people gossip and stir up all kinds of questions. And I don't think I can face them. Or rather, I don't want to face them. Please don't make me. Don't go,' she said urgently. 'At least, not tonight. Let's pretend that you're my lover, even if it's not true. Let me show my sisters and my family that I'm a grown-up woman who doesn't need their protection any more. I want to break free from their well-meaning intervention, and you're the person who can help me. So help me, Dante. Don't make me face them alone in the morning.'

Dante heard the raw appeal in her voice and realised how difficult that must have been for her to say. She seemed so vulnerable that part of him wanted to go over there and comfort her. To cradle her in his arms and tell her everything was going to be all right. But he couldn't do that with any degree of certainty, could he? He didn't even trust himself to touch her without going back on his word and it was vital he kept to his self-imposed promise.

'This is a crazy situation,' he growled. 'Which is going to get even crazier if I stay. I'm sorry, Willow—but I can't do it.'

In the distance, the music suddenly came to a

halt and the sound of clapping drifted in through the open windows.

'But I still have your bag,' she said quietly. 'And I thought you badly wanted it back.'

There was a pause.

'Are you...*threatening* me?' he questioned.

She shrugged. 'I thought we had a deal.'

He met her grey gaze and an unwilling feeling of admiration flooded through him as he realised that she meant it. And even though she wouldn't have had a leg to stand on if he had decided to offer *real* resistance, he knew he couldn't do it. Because there were only so many setbacks a person could take—and she'd had more than her fair share of them.

'Okay,' he said at last. 'The deal still stands, though the terms have changed. And this is what we're going to do. You are going to get ready for bed in the bathroom and you're going to wear something—anything—I don't care what it is as long as it covers you up. You are then going to get into bed and I don't want to hear another word from you until morning, when we will leave for London before anyone else is awake, because I have no intention of facing your family first thing and having to continue with this ridiculous farce.'

'But…where will you sleep?'

With a faint feeling of disbelief that he should be consigning himself to a celibate night, he pointed to a faded velvet chaise longue on the opposite side of the room. 'Over there,' he said.

'Dante…'

'No,' he said, his patience dwindling as he moved away from her, because despite the fact that she was swaddled beneath that fat, white duvet, the image of her slender body wearing nothing but her bra and pants was seared into his memory. He swallowed. 'I want you to do that right now, or the deal is off—and if I have to drive myself back to London and break into your apartment in order to retrieve what is rightfully mine, then I will do it. Do you understand, Willow?'

She met his eyes and nodded with an obedience which somehow made his heart twist.

'Yes, Dante,' she said. 'I understand.'

CHAPTER SIX

THE STRONG SMELL of coffee filtered into her senses, waking Willow from her restless night. Slowly, her eyelids flickered open to see Dante standing by her bed with a steaming mug in his hand. He was already dressed, though looked as if he could do with a shave, because his jaw was dark and shadowed.

So were his eyes.

'Where did you find the coffee?' she asked.

'Where do you think I found it? In the kitchen. And before you ask, the answer is no. Everyone else in the house must be sleeping off their hangover because I didn't bump into anyone else along the way.'

Willow nodded. It was like a bad dream. Actually, it was more like a nightmare. She'd spent the night alone in her childhood bed, covered up in a baggy T-shirt and a pair of pants, while Dante slept on the chaise longue on the other side of the room.

Pushing her hair away from her face, she sat up and stared out of the windows. Neither of them had drawn the drapes last night and the pale blue of the morning sky was edged with puffy little white clouds. The birds were singing fit to burst and the powerful scent of roses drifted in on the still-cool air. It was an English morning at its loveliest and yet its beauty seemed to mock her. It reminded her of all the things she didn't have. All the things she probably never *would* have. It made her think about the disaster of the wedding the day before. She thought about her sister laughing up at her new husband with love shining from her eyes. About the youngest flower girl, clutching her posy with dimpled fists. About the tiny wail of a baby in the church, and the shushing noises of her mother as she'd carried the crying infant outside, to the understanding smiles of the other women present, like they were all members of that exclusive club called *Mothers*.

A twist of pain like a knife in her heart momentarily caught Willow off-guard and it took a moment before she had composed herself enough to turn to look into Dante's bright blue eyes.

'What time is it?' she asked.

'Still early.' His iced gaze swept over her. 'How long will it take you to get ready?'

'Not long.'

'Good,' he said, putting the coffee down on the bedside table and then walking over to the other side of the room to stare out of the window. 'Then just do it, and let's get going as soon as possible, shall we?'

It was couched as a question but there was no disguising the fact that it was another command.

'What about my parents?'

'Leave them a note.'

She wanted to tell him that her mother would hit the roof if she just slunk away without even having breakfast, but she guessed what his response would be. He would shrug and tell her she was welcome to stay. And she didn't *want* to stay here, without him. She wanted to keep her pathetic fantasy alive for a while longer. She wanted people to see what wasn't really true. Willow with her boyfriend. Willow who'd just spent the night with a devastatingly attractive man. Lucky Willow.

Only she wasn't lucky at all, was she?

Sliding out of bed, she grabbed her clothes and took the quickest shower on record as she tried very hard not to think about the way she'd pleaded with Dante to have sex with her the night before. Or the way he'd turned her down. He'd told her it was because he was cold and sometimes cruel. He'd told her he didn't want to hurt her and maybe that was thoughtfulness on his part—how ironic, then, that he had ended up by hurting her anyway.

Dressing in jeans and a T-shirt and twisting her hair into a single plait, Willow returned to the bedroom, drank her cooled coffee and then walked with Dante through the blessedly quiet corridors towards the back of the house.

She should have realised it was too good to be true, because there, standing by the kitchen door wearing a silky dressing gown and a pair of flip-flops, stood her mother. Willow stared at her in dismay. Had she heard her and Dante creeping through the house, or was this yet another example of the finely tuned antennae her mother always seemed able to call upon whenever she was around?

'M-Mum,' stumbled Willow awkwardly.

A pair of eyebrows were arched in her direction. 'Going somewhere?'

Willow felt her cheeks grow pink and was racking her brains about what to say, when Dante intercepted.

'You must forgive us for slipping away so early after such a fabulous day yesterday, Mrs Hamilton—but I have a pile of work I need to get through before I go back to Paris and Willow has promised to help me.' He smiled. 'Haven't you?'

Willow had never seen her mother look quite so flustered—but how could she possibly object in the face of all that undeniable charm and charisma Dante was directing at her? She saw the quick flare of hope in her mother's eyes. Was she in danger of projecting into the future, just as Great-aunt Maud had done last night?

Kissing her mother goodbye she and Dante went outside, but during the short time she'd spent getting ready, the puffy white clouds had accumulated and spread across the sky like foam on a cup of macchiato. Suddenly, the air had a distinct chill and Willow shivered as Dante put the car roof up and she slid onto the passenger seat.

It wasn't like the outward journey, when the wind had rushed through their hair and the sun had shone and she had been filled with a distinct sensation of hope and excitement. Enclosed beneath the soft roof, the atmosphere felt claustrophobic and tense and the roar of his powerful car sounded loud as it broke the early-morning Sunday silence.

They drove for a little way without saying anything, and once out on the narrow, leafy lanes, Willow risked a glance at him. His dark hair curled very slightly over the collar of his shirt and his olive skin glowed. Despite his obvious lack of sleep and being in need of a shave, he looked healthy and glowing—like a man at the very peak of his powers, but his profile was set and unmoving.

She cleared her throat. 'Are you angry with me?'

Dante stared straight ahead as the hedgerows passed in a blur of green. He'd spent an unendurable night. Not just because his six-foot-plus frame had dwarfed the antique piece of furniture on which he'd been attempting to sleep, but because he'd felt bad. And it hadn't got any better. He'd been forced to listen to Willow tossing and turning while she slept. To imagine that pale and slender body moving restlessly against the sheet. He'd remembered how she'd felt. How she'd tasted. How she'd begged him to make love to her. He had been filled with a heady sexual hunger which had made him want to explode. He'd wanted her, and yet rejecting her had been his only honourable choice. Because what he'd said had been true. He *did* hurt women. He'd never found one who was capable of chipping her way through the stony walls he'd erected around his heart, and sometimes he didn't think he ever would. And in the meantime, Willow Hamilton needed protection from a man like him.

'I'm angry with myself,' he said.

'Because?'

'Because I should have chosen a less controversial way of getting my bag back. I shouldn't have agreed to be your plus one.' He gave a short laugh. 'But you were very persuasive.'

She didn't answer immediately. He could see her finger drawing little circles over one of the peacocks which adorned her denim-covered thigh.

'There must be something in that bag you want very badly.'

'There is.'

'But I don't suppose you're going to tell me what it is?'

The car had slowed down to allow a stray sheep to pick its way laboriously across the road, giving them a slightly dazed glance as it did so. Dante's instinct was to tell her that her guess was correct, but suddenly he found himself wanting to tell her. Was that because so far he hadn't discussed it with anyone? Because he and his twin brother were estranged and he wasn't particularly close to any of his other siblings? That all their dark secrets and their heartache seemed to have pushed them all apart, rather than bringing them closer together...

'The bag contains a diamond and emerald tiara,' he said. 'Worth hundreds of thousands of dollars.'

Her finger stopped moving. 'You're kidding?'

'No, I'm not. My grandfather specifically asked

me to get it for him and it took me weeks to track the damned thing down. He calls it one of his Lost Mistresses, for reasons he's reluctant to explain. He sold it a long time ago and now he wants it back.'

'Do you know why?'

He shrugged. 'Maybe because he's dying.'

'I'm sorry,' she said softly, and he wondered if she'd heard the slight break in his voice.

'Yeah,' he said gruffly, his tightened lips intended to show her that the topic was now closed.

They drove for a while in silence and had just hit the outskirts of greater London, when her voice broke into his thoughts.

'Your name is Italian,' she commented quietly. 'But your accent isn't. Sometimes you sound American, but at other times your accent could almost be Italian, or French. How come?'

Dante thought how women always wanted to do things the wrong way round. Shouldn't she have made chatty little enquiries about his background *before* he'd had his hand inside her panties yesterday? And yet wasn't he grateful that she'd moved from the subject of his family?

'Because I was born in the States,' he said. 'And spent the first eight years of my life there—until I was sent away to boarding school in Europe.'

She nodded and he half expected the usual squeak of indignation. Because women invariably thought they were showcasing their caring side by professing horror at the thought of a little boy being sent away from home so young. But he remembered that the English were different and her aristocratic class in particular had always sent young boys away to school.

'And did you like it?' she questioned.

Dante nodded, knowing his reaction had been unusual—the supposition being that any child would hate being removed from the heart of their family. Except in his case there hadn't been a heart. That had been torn out one dark and drug-fuelled night—shattered and smashed—leaving behind nothing but emptiness, anger and guilt.

'As it happens, I liked it very much,' he drawled, deliberately pushing the bitter thoughts away. 'It was in the Swiss mountains—pure and white and unbelievably beautiful.' He paused as he remembered how the soft white flakes used to swarm down from the sky, blanketing the world in a pure silence—and how he had eagerly retreated into that cold space where nothing or nobody could touch him. 'We used to ski every day, which wore us out so much that there wasn't really time to think. And there were kids from all over the world, so it was kind of anonymous—and I liked that.'

'You must speak another language.'

'I speak three others,' he said. 'French, Italian and German.'

'And that's why you live in Paris?'

His mouth hardened. 'I don't remember mentioning that I lived in Paris.'

Out of the corner of his eye he saw her shoulders slump a little.

'I must have read that on the internet too. You

can't blame me,' she said, her words leaving her mouth in a sudden rush.

'No, I don't blame you,' he said. Just as he couldn't blame her for the sudden sexual tension which seemed to have sprung up between them again, which was making it difficult for him to concentrate. Maybe that was inevitable. They were two people who'd been interrupted while making out, leaving them both aching and frustrated. And even though his head was telling him that was the best thing which could have happened, his body seemed to have other ideas.

Because right now all he could think about was how soft her skin had felt as he had skated his fingertips all the way up beneath that flouncy little dress she'd been wearing. He remembered the slenderness of her hips and breasts as she'd stood before him in her bra and panties—defiant yet innocent as she'd stripped off her bridesmaid dress and let it pool around her feet. He'd resisted her then, even though the scent of her arousal had called out to his hungry body on a primitive level which had made resistance almost unendurable. Was that what was happening now? Why he wanted to stop the car and take her somewhere—anywhere—so that he could be alone with her? Free to pull aside her clothes. To unzip her jeans and tease her until she was writhing in helpless appeal.

He wondered if he'd been out of his mind to say no. He could easily have introduced her to limitless pleasures in his arms—and what better initiation for a virgin than lovemaking with someone like him? But it wasn't his technique which was in question, but his inbuilt emotional distance. He couldn't connect. He didn't know how.

'So why Paris?' she was asking.

Make her get the message, he thought. *Make her realise that she's had a lucky escape from a man like you.*

'It's well placed for central Europe,' he said. 'I like the city and the food and the culture. And, of course, the women,' he added deliberately. 'French women are very easy to like.'

'I can imagine they must be,' she said, her voice sounding unnaturally bright.

The car was soon swallowed up by the heavier London traffic and he noticed she was staring fixedly out of the window.

'We're nearly here,' he said, forcing himself to make some conversational remark. To try to draw a line under this as neatly as possible. 'So…have you got any plans for the rest of the day?'

Willow gazed at the familiar wide streets close to her apartment and realised he was preparing to say goodbye to her. What she would like to do more than anything else was to rail against the unfairness of it all. Not only had he turned her down, but he'd deliberately started talking about other women—*French women*—as if to drive home just how forgettable she really was. And he had done it just as she'd been speculating about his fast, international lifestyle. Thinking that he didn't seem like the sort of man who would ever embrace the role of husband and father…the sort of man who really would have been a perfect lover for a woman like her.

Well, she was just going to have to forget her stupid daydreams. Just tick it off and put it down to experience. She would get over it, as she had got over so much else. No way was she going to leave him with an enduring memory of her behaving like a victim. *Remember how he moaned in your arms when he kissed you*, she reminded herself fiercely as she slanted him a smile. *Remember that* you *have some power here, too.*

'I'll probably go for a walk in Regent's Park,' she said. 'The flowers are gorgeous at this time of the year. And I might meet a friend later and catch a film. How about you?'

'I'll pick up my bag from you and then fly straight back to France.' He stifled a yawn. 'It's been an eventful few days.'

And that, thought Willow, was that.

She was glad of all the times when her mother had drummed in the importance of posture because it meant that she was able to walk into her apartment with her head held very proud and her shoulders as stiff as a ramrod, as Dante followed her inside.

She pulled out the leather case from the bottom of her wardrobe, her fingers closing around it just before she handed it to him.

'I'd love to see the tiara,' she said.

He shook his head. 'Better not.'

'Even though I inadvertently carried a priceless piece of jewellery through customs without declaring it?'

'You shouldn't have picked up the wrong bag.'

You shouldn't have been distracting me. 'And I could now be languishing in some jail somewhere,' she continued.

He gave a slow smile. 'I would have bailed you out.'

'I only have your word for that,' she said.

'And you don't trust my word?'

She shrugged. 'I don't know you well enough to answer that. Besides, oughtn't you to check that the piece is intact? That I haven't substituted something fake in its place—or stolen one of the stones. That this Lost Mistress is in a decent state to give to your grandfather and...'

But her words died away as he began to unlock the leather case and slowly drew out a jewelled tiara—a glittering coronet of white diamonds and almond-size emeralds as green as new leaves. Against Dante's olive skin they sparked their bright fire and it was impossible for Willow to look anywhere else but at them.

'Oh, but they're beautiful,' she breathed. 'Just beautiful.'

Her eyes were shining as she said it and something about her unselfconscious appreciation touched something inside him. And Dante felt a funny twist of regret as he said goodbye. As if he was walking away from something unfinished. It seemed inappropriate to shake her hand, yet he didn't trust himself to kiss her cheek, for he suspected that even the lightest touch would rekindle his desire. He would send her flowers as a thank-you, he decided. Maybe even a diamond on a fine gold chain—you couldn't go wrong with something like that. She'd be able to show it off to her sisters and pretend that their relationship had been real. And one day she would be grateful to him for his restraint. She would accept the truth of what he'd said and realise that someone like him would bring her nothing but heartache. She would find herself some suitable English aristocrat and move to a big house in the country where she could live a life not unlike that of her parents.

He didn't turn on his phone until he was at the airfield because he despised people who allowed themselves to get distracted on the road. But he wished afterwards that he'd checked his messages while he was closer to Willow's apartment. Close enough to go back for a showdown.

As it was, he drove to the airfield in a state of blissful ignorance, and the first he knew about the disruption was when his assistant, René, rushed up to him brandishing a newspaper—a look of astonishment contorting his Gallic features.

'*C'est impossible!* Why didn't you tell me, boss?' he accused. 'I have been trying to get hold of you all morning, wondering what you want me to say to the press…'

'Why should I want you to say anything to the press?' demanded Dante impatiently. 'When you know how much I hate them.'

His assistant gave a flamboyant shake of his head. 'I think their sudden interest is understandable, in the circumstances.'

Dante frowned. 'What the hell are you talking about?'

'It is everywhere!' declared René. 'Absolutely everywhere! All of Paris is buzzing with the news that the bad-boy American playboy has fallen in love at last—and that you are engaged to an English aristocrat called Willow Anoushka Hamilton.'

CHAPTER SEVEN

WILLOW FELT RESTLESS after Dante had left, unable to settle to anything. Distractedly, she wandered around her apartment—except that never had it felt more like living in someone else's space than it did right then. It seemed as if the charismatic American had invaded the quiet rooms and left something of himself behind. She couldn't seem to stop thinking about his bright blue eyes and hard body and the plummeting of her heart as he'd said goodbye.

She slipped on a pair of sneakers and let herself outside, but for once the bright colours of the immaculate flower beds in the nearby park were wasted on her. It was funny how your thoughts could keep buzzing and buzzing around your head, just like the pollen-laden bees which were

clinging like crazy to stop themselves from top-
pling off the delicate blooms.

She thought about the chaste night she'd spent
with Dante. She thought about the way he'd
kissed her and the way she'd been kissed in the
past. But up until now she'd always clammed
up whenever a man touched her. She'd started
to believe that she wasn't capable of real pas-
sion. That maybe she was incapable of reacting
like a normal woman. But Dante Di Sione had
awoken something in her the moment he'd
touched her. *And then walked away just because
she'd been ill as a kid.*

She bought a pint of milk on her way home
from the park and was in the kitchen making
coffee when the loud shrill of the doorbell pen-
etrated the uncomfortable swirl of her thoughts.
She wasn't really concentrating when she went
into the hall to see who it was, startled to see
Dante standing on her doorstep with a look on
his face she couldn't quite work out.

She blinked at him, aware of the thunder of her

heart and the need to keep her reaction hidden. To try to hide the sudden flash of hope inside her. Had he changed his mind? Did he realise that he only had to say the word and she would be sliding between the sheets with him—right now, if he wanted her?

'Did you forget something?' she said, but the dark expression on his face quickly put paid to any lingering hope. And then he was brushing past her, that brief contact only adding to her sense of disorientation. 'What do you think you're doing?'

'Shut the door,' he said tersely.

'You can't just walk in here and start telling me what to do.'

'Shut the door, Willow,' he repeated grimly. 'Unless you want your neighbours to hear what I have to say.'

Part of her wanted to challenge him. To tell him to go right ahead and that she didn't care what her neighbours thought. Because he didn't want her, did he? He'd rejected her—so what right did he have to start throwing his weight around like this?

Yet he looked so golden and gorgeous as he towered over her, dominating the shaded entrance hall of the basement apartment, that it was difficult for her to think straight. And suddenly she couldn't bear to be this close without wanting to reach out and touch him. To trace her finger along the dark graze of his jaw and drift it upwards to his lips. *So start taking control*, she told herself fiercely. *This is* your *home and* he's *the trespasser. Don't let him tell you what you should or shouldn't do.*

'I was just making coffee,' she said with an airiness which belied her pounding heart as she headed off towards the kitchen, aware that he was very close behind her. She willed her hand to stay steady as she poured herself a mug and then flicked him an enquiring gaze. 'Would you like one?'

'I haven't come for coffee.'

'Then why *have* you come here, with a look on your face which would turn the milk sour?'

His fists clenched by the faded denim of his powerful thighs and his features darkened. 'What did you hope to achieve by this, Willow?' he hissed. 'Did you imagine that your petulant display would be enough to get you what you wanted, and that I'd take you to bed despite my better judgement?'

She stared at him. 'I don't know what you're talking about.'

'Oh, really?'

'Yes. *Really.*'

'So you have no idea why it's all over the internet that you and I are engaged to be married?'

Willow could feel all the blood drain from her face. 'No, of course I didn't!' And then her hand flew to her lips. 'Unless...'

'So you do know?' he demanded, firing the words at her like bullets.

Please let me wake up, Willow thought. *Let me close my eyes, and when I open them again he*

*will have disappeared and this will have been
nothing but a bad dream.*

But it wasn't and he hadn't. He was still standing there glaring at her, only now his expression
had changed from being a potential milk-curdler,
to looking as if he would like to put his hands on
her shoulders and throttle her.

'I may have…' She took a deep breath. 'I was
talking to my sister about you—or rather, she
was interrogating me about you. She asked if we
were serious and I tried to be vague—and my
aunt overheard us, and started getting carried
away with talking about weddings and I didn't…
well, I didn't bother to correct her.'

His eyes narrowed. 'And why would you do
something like that?' he questioned dangerously.

Why?

Willow met his accusing gaze and something
inside her flared like a small and painful flame.
Couldn't he see? Didn't he realise that the reasons were heartbreakingly simple. Because for
once she'd felt like she was part of the real world,

instead of someone just watching from the side-lines. Because she'd allowed herself to start believing in her own fantasy.

'I didn't realise it was going to get out of hand like this,' she said. 'And I'm sorry.'

'You're *sorry*?' he repeated incredulously. 'You think a couple of mumbled words of apology and everything's going to go back to normal?' His face darkened again. 'My assistant has been fielding phone calls all morning and my Paris office has been inundated with reporters asking for a comment. I'm in the process of brokering a deal with a man who is fiercely private and yet it seems as if I am about to be surrounded by my own personal press pack. How do you think that's going to look?'

'Can't you just…issue a denial?'

Dante stared into her soft grey eyes and felt close to exploding. 'You think it's that simple?'

'We could say that I was… I don't know…' Helplessly, Willow shrugged. *'Joking?'*

His mouth hardened, and now there was something new in his eyes. Something dark. Something bleak.

'A denial might have worked, were it not for the fact that some enterprising journalist was alerted to the Di Sione name and decided to telephone my grandfather's house on Long Island to ask him for his reaction.' His blue eyes sparked with fury as they captured hers with their shuttered gaze. 'And despite the time difference between here and New York, it just so happened that my grandfather was suffering from insomnia and boredom and pain, and was more than willing to accept the call. Which is why…'

He paused, as if he was only just hanging on to his temper by a shred.

'Why I received a call from the old man, telling me how pleased he is that I'm settling down at last. Telling me how lovely you are—and what a good family you come from. I was trying to find the right moment to tell him that there is nothing going on between us, only the right moment didn't seem to come—or rather, my grandfather didn't give me a chance to say what I wanted to.'

'Dante...'

'Don't you *dare* interrupt me when I haven't finished,' he ground out. 'Because using the kind of shameless emotional blackmail he has always used to ensure he gets his own way, my grandfather then told me how much *better* he'd felt when he heard the news. He said he hadn't felt this good in a long time and that it was high time I took myself a wife.'

'I'm sorry.' She gave him a beseeching look. 'What else can I say?'

Dante felt a feeling of pure rage flood through him and wondered how he could have been stupid enough to take his eye off the ball. Or had he forgotten what women were really like—had he completely wiped Lucy from his memory? Had it conveniently slipped his mind that the so-called *fairer sex* were manipulative and devious and would stop at nothing to get what it was they wanted? How easy it was to forget the past when you had been bewitched by a supposedly shy blonde and a sob story about needing a temporary date which had convinced him to go to the damned wedding in the first place.

He stared at the slight quiver of Willow's lips and at that moment he understood for the first time in his life the meaning of the term *a punishing kiss*, because that was what he wanted to do to her right now. He wanted to punish her for screwing up his plans with her thoughtlessness and her careless tongue. He watched as a slow colour crept up to inject her creamy skin with a faint blush, and felt his body harden. Come to think of it, he'd like to punish her every which way. He'd like to lay her down and flatten her against the floor and…and…

'Are you one of those habitual fantasists?' he demanded hotly. 'One of those women who goes around pretending to be something she isn't, to make herself seem more interesting?'

She put her coffee cup down so suddenly that some of it slopped over the side, but she didn't even seem to notice. Her hands gripped the edge of the table, as if she needed its weathered wooden surface for support.

'That's an unfair thing to say,' she breathed.

'Why? Because you're so delicate and precious that I'm not allowed to tell the truth?' He gave a short laugh. 'I thought you despised being given special treatment just because you'd been ill. Well, you can't have it both ways, Willow. You can't play the shrinking violet whenever it suits you—and a feisty modern woman the next. You need to decide who you really are.'

She met his eyes in the silence which followed. 'You certainly don't pull your punches, do you?'

'I'm treating you the same as I would any other woman.'

'Oh, but that's where you're wrong, because you're not!' she said with a shake of her head. 'If I was any other woman, you would have had sex with me last night. You know you would.'

Dante felt the heavy beat of a pulse at his temple and silently cursed her for bringing that up again. Did she think she would wear him down with her persistence? That what Willow wanted, Willow would get. His mouth hardened, but unfortunately, so did his groin. 'Like I told you. I don't sleep with virgins.'

She turned away, but not before he noticed the dark flare of colour which washed over her cheekbones and he felt his anger morph inconveniently into lust. How easy it would be to vent his feelings by giving her what she wanted. What he wanted. Even now. Despite the accusations he'd hurled at her and the still-unsettled question of how her indiscretion was going to be resolved, it was sexual tension which dominated the air so powerfully that he couldn't hardly breathe without choking on it. He couldn't seem to tear his gaze away from her. She looked as brittle as glass as she held her shoulders stiffly, and although she was staring out of the small basement window, he was willing to lay a bet she didn't see a thing.

But he did. He saw plenty. He could see the slender swell of her bottom beneath the dark denim. He could see the silken cascade of her blond hair as it spilled down her back. Would it make him feel better if he went right over there and slid down her jeans, and laid her down on the kitchen table and straddled her, before feasting on her?

He swallowed as an aching image of her pale, parted thighs flashed vividly into his mind and he felt another powerful tug of desire. On one level, of *course* it would make them both feel better, but on another—what? He would be stirring up yet more consequences, and weren't there more than enough to be going on with?

She turned back again to face him and he saw that the flush had gone, as if her pale skin had absorbed it, like blotting paper. 'Like I said, I'm sorry, but there's nothing I can do about it now.'

He shook his head. 'But that's where you're wrong, little Miss Hamilton. There *is*.'

Did something alert her to the determination which had hardened his voice? Was that why her eyes had grown so wary?

'What? You want me to write to your grandfather and apologise? And then to give some kind of statement to the press, telling them that it was all a misunderstanding? I'll do all that, if that's what it takes.'

'No. That's not what's going to happen,' he said. 'It's a little more complicated than that. My grandfather wants to meet the woman he thinks I'm going to marry. And you, my dear Willow, are going to embrace that role.'

The grey of her eyes was darker now, as if someone had smudged them with charcoal and a faint frown was criss-crossing over her brow. 'I don't understand.'

'Then let me explain it clearly, so there can be no mistake,' he said. 'My grandfather is a sick man and anything which makes him feel better is fine with me. He wants me to bring you to the family home to meet him and that's exactly what's going to happen. You can play the fantasist for a little while longer because you are coming with me to Long Island. As my fiancée.'

CHAPTER EIGHT

A SOFT BREEZE wafted in through the open windows, making the filmy drapes at the window shiver like a bridal veil and the mocking significance of *that* didn't escape Willow. She drew her hand over her clammy brow and looked around the luxurious room. She could hardly believe she was here, on Dante's estate, or that he had persuaded her to come here for a long weekend, despite the many objections she'd raised.

But he'd made her feel guilty—and guilt was a powerful motivator. He'd said that her lies about being his fiancée had given his grandfather hope, and it was in her power to ensure that a dying man's hopes were not dashed.

'You seemed to want to let your family believe that you were going to be my bride,' were his exact, silken words. 'Well, now this is your chance to play the role for real.'

Except that it wasn't real, because a real bride-to-be would be cherished and caressed by her fiancé, wouldn't she? Not kept at a chilly distance as if she was something unwanted but necessary—like a bandage you might be forced to wrap around an injured arm.

They were installed in an unbelievably cute cottage in the extensive grounds, but in a way that was worse than staying in the main house. Because in here there was the illusion of intimacy, while in reality they were two people who couldn't have been further apart. She was closeted alone with a man who clearly despised her. And there was only one bed. Willow swallowed. This time it was a king-size bed, but the principle of where to sleep remained the same. Was he really willing to repeat what had happened at the wedding—sharing a bedroom, while keeping his distance from her?

Dante had telephoned ahead to tell the housekeeper that they wished to be guaranteed privacy.

She remembered the look on his face as he'd finished the call. 'They'll think it's because we're crazy about each other and can't keep our hands off each other,' he'd said mockingly.

But Willow knew the real reason. It meant that they wouldn't be forced to continue with the farce for any longer than necessary. There would be no reason for Dante to hide his undeniable hostility towards her. When they were with other people they would be sweetness and light together, while in private…

She bit her lip, trying hard to block out the sound of the powerful shower jets from the en-suite bathroom and not to think about Dante standing naked beneath them, but it wasn't easy. Their enforced proximity had made her achingly aware of him—whether he was in the same room, or not.

They had flown in by helicopter an hour earlier and Willow's first sight of the Di Sione family home had taken her breath away. She'd grown up in a big home, yes—but this was nothing like the crumbling house in which she'd spent her own formative years. This, she'd realised, was what real wealth looked like. It was solid and real, and clearly money was no object. The white marble of the Long Island mansion was gleaming and so pristine that she couldn't imagine anyone actually *living* in it. She had been aware of the endless sweep of emerald lawns, the turquoise flash of a swimming pool and the distant glitter of a huge lake as their helicopter had landed.

A housekeeper named Alma had welcomed them and told Dante that his grandfather was sleeping but looking forward to seeing them both at dinner.

'And your sister is here, of course,' she said.

'Talia?' questioned Dante as the housekeeper nodded.

'That's right. She's out making sketches for a new painting.' Alma had given Willow a friendly smile. 'You'll meet Miss Natalia at dinner.'

And Willow had nodded and tried to look as she thought a newly engaged woman *should* look—and not like someone who had recently been handed a diamond ring by Dante, with all the emotion of someone producing a cheap trinket from the remains of a Christmas cracker.

'What's this?' she'd asked as he had deposited a small velvet box on her lap.

'Your number one prop,' came his mocking response as their helicopter had hovered over the Di Sione landing pad. 'The bling. That thing which women love to flash as a symbol of success—the outward sign that they've *got their man.*'

'What an unbelievably cynical thing to say.'

'You think it's cynical to tell the truth?' he'd demanded. 'Or are you denying that women view the acquisition of diamonds as if it's some new kind of competitive sport?'

The awful thing was that Willow secretly agreed with him. Her sisters were crazy about diamonds—and so were plenty of the women she worked with—yet she'd always found them a cold and emotionless stone. The giant solitaire winked at her now like some malevolent foe, splashing rainbow fire over her pale fingers as Dante emerged from the bathroom.

Quickly, she looked up, her heart beginning to pound. She'd been half expecting him to emerge wearing nothing but a towel slung around his hips, and guessed she should be pleased that he must have dressed in the bathroom. But her overriding sensation was one of disappointment. Had she secretly been hoping to catch a glimpse of that magnificent olive body as he patted himself dry? Was there some masochistic urge lurking inside her which wanted to taunt her with what she hadn't got?

Yet the dark trousers and silk shirt he wore did little to disguise his muscular physique and his fully dressed state did nothing to dim his powerful air of allure. His black hair was still damp and his eyes looked intensely blue, and suddenly Willow felt her heart lurch with a dizzying yet wasted sense of desire. Because since that interrupted seduction at her sister's wedding, he hadn't touched her. Not once. He had avoided all physical contact with the studied exaggeration of someone in the military walking through a field studded with landmines.

His gaze flickered to where she'd been studying her hand and his eyes gleamed with mockery. As if he'd caught her gloating. 'Do you like your ring?'

'It looks way too big on my hand,' she said truthfully. 'And huge solitaire diamonds aren't really my thing.'

He raised his dark brows mockingly, as if he didn't quite believe her.

'But they have a much better resale value than something bespoke,' he drawled.

'Of course,' she said, and then a rush of nerves washed over her as she thought about the reality of going to dinner that evening and playing the part of his intended bride. 'You know, if we're planning to convince your grandfather that we really are a couple, then I'm going to need to know something about you. And if you could try being a little less hostile towards me that might help.'

He slipped a pair of heavy gold cufflinks in place and clipped them closed before answering. 'What exactly do you want to know?'

She wanted to know why he was so cynical. And why his face had darkened as soon as the helicopter had landed here today.

'You told me about being sent away to boarding school in Switzerland, but you didn't say why.'

'Does there have to be a reason?'

She hesitated. 'I'm thinking that maybe there was. And if there was, then I would probably know about it.'

Dante's instinct was to snap out some terse response—the familiar blocking technique he used whenever questions strayed into the territory of *personal*. Because he didn't trust personal. He didn't trust anyone or anything, and Willow Hamilton was no exception in the trust stakes, with her manipulation and evasion. But suddenly her face had become soft with what looked like genuine concern and he felt a tug of something unfamiliar deep inside him. An inexplicable urge to colour in some of the blank spaces of his past. Was that because he wanted his grandfather to die happy by convincing him that he'd found true love at last? Or because— despite her careless tongue landing them in this ridiculous situation—she possessed a curious sense of vulnerability which somehow managed to burrow beneath his defences.

His lips tightened as he reminded himself how clever Giovanni was. How he would see through a fake engagement in the blinking of an eye if he wasn't careful. So tell her, he thought. She was right. He should tell her the stuff which any fiancée would expect to know.

'I'm one of seven children,' he said, shooting out the facts like bullets. 'And my grandfather stepped in to care for us when my parents died very suddenly.'

'And...how did they die?'

'Violently,' he answered succinctly.

Her eyes clouded and Dante saw comprehension written in their soft, grey depths. As if she understood pain. And he didn't want her to *understand*. He wanted her to nod as he presented her with the bare facts—not look at him as if he was some kind of problem she could solve.

Yet there had been times when he'd longed for someone to work their magic on him. He stared out at the distant glitter of the lake. To find a woman he'd be happy to go to bed with, night after night—instead of suffering from chronic boredom as soon as anyone tried to get close to him. To find some kind of *peace* with another human being—the kind of peace which seemed almost unimaginable to him. Was that how his twin had felt about Anais? he wondered.

He thought about Dario and felt the bitter twist of remorse as he remembered what he had done to his brother.

'What exactly happened?' Willow was asking.

Her gentle tone threatened to undermine his resolve. Making him want to show her what his life had been like. To show her that she didn't have the monopoly on difficult childhoods. And suddenly, it was like a dam breaking through and flooding him.

'My father was a screwed-up hedonist,' he said bluntly. 'A kid with too much money who saw salvation in the bottom of a bottle, or in the little pile of white dust he snorted through a hundred dollar bill.' His lips tightened. 'He blamed his addictions on the fact that my grandfather had never been there for him when he was growing up—but plenty of people have absent parents and don't end up having to live their lives on a constant high.'

'And what about your mother?' she questioned as calmly as if he'd just been telling her that his father had been president of the Union.

He shook his head. 'She was cut from the same cloth. Or maybe he taught her to be that way—I don't know. All I do know is that she liked the feeling of being out of her head as well. Or maybe she needed to blot out the reality, because my father wasn't exactly known for his fidelity. Their parties were legendary. I remember I used to creep downstairs to find it looking like some kind of Roman orgy, with people lying around among the empty bottles and glasses and the sounds of women gasping in the pool house. And then one day my mother just stopped. She started seeing a therapist and went into rehab, and although she replaced the drink and the drugs with a shopping addiction, for a while everything was…' He shrugged as he struggled to find a word which would sum up the chaos of his family life.

'Normal?'

He gave a short and bitter laugh. 'No, Willow. It was never normal, but it was better. In fact, for a while it was great. We felt we'd got our mother back. And then…'

'Then?' she prompted again.

He wasn't even angry with her for her persistence because now it felt like some rank poison was throbbing beneath his skin and he needed to cut through the surface to let that poison out.

'One night there was some big row. I don't

know what it was about—all I do know is that my father was completely loaded and my mother was shouting at him. I heard him yell back that he was going out and then I heard her going after him. I knew he was in no state to drive and I tried to stop her. I…'

He'd done more than try. He'd begged her not to go. He'd run over and clung to her with all the strength his eight-year-old body could muster, but she hadn't listened. She'd got in the car anyway and the next time he'd seen his mother was when she'd been laid out in her coffin, with white lilies in her hands and that waxy look on her cold, cold cheeks.

'She wouldn't listen to me,' he bit out. 'He crashed the car and killed them both. And I didn't manage to stop her. Even though deep down I knew what a state my father was in, I let her go.'

He stared out at the grounds of the house he'd moved into soon afterwards when his grandfather had brought them all here. A place where he'd been unable to shake off his sorrow and his guilt. He'd run wild until his grandfather had sent him and Dario away to school. And he'd just kept on running, hadn't he? He wondered now if the failure of his attempt to stop his mother had been the beginning of his fierce need to control. The reason why he always felt compelled to step in and influence what was happening around him. Was that why he'd done what he'd done to his twin brother?

'But maybe you couldn't stop her.'

Willow's voice—suddenly so strong and sure—broke into his thoughts.

'What are you talking about?' he demanded.

'Children can't always make adults behave the way they want them to, Dante,' she said, her words washing over him like balm. 'No matter how hard they try.'

Dante turned round, still unable to believe how much she'd got out of him. She looked like some kind of angel sitting there, with her pale English skin and that waterfall of silky hair. In her simple cotton dress she looked so pure—hell, she *was* pure. But it was more than just about sex. She looked as if she could take all the darkness away from him and wash away the stain of guilt from his heart. And her grey eyes were fixed on him, quite calmly—as if she knew exactly what was going on inside his head and was silently urging him to go right ahead and do it.

He wasn't thinking as he walked across the room to where she sat at an antique writing desk with the oil painting of Sicily which hung on the wall behind it. The hot, scorched brushstrokes and cerulean blue of the sky contrasted vividly with her coolness. Her lips looked soft and inviting. Some warning bell was sounding inside his head, telling him that this was wrong. But some of the poison had left him now. Left him feeling empty and aching and wanting her. Wanting to lose himself in her.

She didn't object when he pulled her out of the chair and onto her feet. In fact, the sudden yearning in her eyes suggested that she'd wanted him to touch her just as badly as he needed to.

His hands were in her hair and his mouth was hovering over hers, their lips not quite touching, as if he'd had a last-minute moment of sanity and this was his chance to pull back from her. Was that why she stood up on tiptoe and anchored her hands to his shoulders? Why she flickered the tip of her tongue inside his mouth?

'Willow,' he whispered as his heart began to pound.

'Yes,' she whispered back. 'I'm right here.'

He groaned as he tasted her—his senses tantalised by the faint drift of her scent. Dropping his hands from her hair, he gripped her waist and he thought how incredibly *light* she felt. As light as those drifts of swansdown you sometimes saw floating across hazy summer lawns. He deepened the kiss, and as she sucked in a breath, it felt like she was sucking him right inside her. For a moment he thought about the very obvious place where he would like to *be* sucked and his hand reached down to cup her breast. He heard the urgent little sigh of delight she made.

He felt the restless circle of her narrow hips, and he could feel control leaving him as she kissed him back. He tried to remember where he'd put his condoms and just how long they had before they were expected up at the main house. And all the time he could feel himself going under— as if he was being consumed by a tide of rich, dark honey.

But along with the sweet, sharp kick of desire came the reminder of all the things he'd told himself he wasn't going to do. He'd messed up enough in his life. He'd failed to save his mother. He'd ruptured his relationship with his twin brother. In business he'd achieved outstanding success, but his personal relationships were not the same. Everything he touched turned to dust. He was incapable of experiencing the emotions which other men seemed to feel. And even though Willow Hamilton had allowed her stupid fantasies to manipulate events… Even though she had dragged him into her fantasy and made

it impossible for him to walk away from her—
that gave him no right to hurt her.

It would be too easy to take her innocence. To
be the first man to claim her body for his own.
To introduce her to the powerful but ultimately
fleeting pleasures of sex. He closed his eyes because imagining her sweet tightness encasing
him was almost too much to bear. He thought
about easing into her molten heat, with his mouth
clamped to one of her tiny nipples. He thought
about how good it would feel to be able to come
inside her. To pump his seed into her until he was
empty and replete. To kiss her and kiss her until
she fell asleep in his arms.

But a woman's virginity was a big deal, and
someone who had suffered as Willow had suffered deserved more than he could ever give her.
Because he was programmed not to trust and
never to stay. He would take pleasure and give
pleasure and then close the door and leave without a backwards glance.

Dragging his mouth away from hers and dropping his hand from her breast as if it was on fire, he stepped away, trying to quieten down the fierce sexual hunger which was burning inside him. But when he saw the confusion clouding her beautiful eyes, he felt a moment of unfamiliar doubt which he couldn't seem to block out.

His mouth twisted.

'I meant what I said back in England,' he gritted. 'You aren't somebody I intend to get intimate with, Willow. Did you think that because I've just told you something about my *deeply troubled* past...' His voice took on a harsh and mocking tone. 'That I would want you? Did you think any of this was for real? Because if you do, you're making a big mistake. For the sake of my grandfather and his romantic ideals, we will play the part of the happily engaged couple whenever we find ourselves in his company. But when we're alone, the reality will be very different. Just so you know, I'll be sleeping on the couch.' He gave a tight smile. 'And I'll do my best not to disturb you.'

CHAPTER NINE

THE DARK SHAPE was moving almost silently around the room but it was enough to disturb Willow from her troubled sleep. Pushing the hair back from her face, she sat up in bed and snapped on the light to see Dante standing fully dressed, his face shadowed and unfriendly.

'What are you doing?' she whispered.

'Going out for a drive.'

'But it's only...' She picked up her watch and blinked at it. 'Just after five in the morning!'

'I know what the time is,' he growled back as he grabbed a clutch of car keys.

'So...why?' Her voice was full of bewilderment as she looked at him. 'Why in heaven's name are you going out before the sun is even up?'

'Why do you think?' He turned to look at her

properly and all his dark and restless energy seemed to wash over her. 'Because I can't sleep.'

Willow swallowed. 'That couch *does* look very uncomfortable,' she agreed carefully. 'It can't be doing your back any good.'

'It's got nothing to do with the damned couch, Willow, and we both know it.'

She leaned back against the pillows, wishing that he would stop snapping at her, and just end this impasse. Wishing he'd just take off those jeans and that stupid jacket and come and get in bed with her and do what was almost driving her out of her mind with longing. How many nights had they spent here now? And still her virginity was intact. Nothing had changed—at least, not in him—though her desire for him was as strong as ever. She wanted to kiss him. She wanted to hold him. Yet he acted as if she was contaminated.

'It was a mistake to come to this damned cottage,' he bit out. 'And an even bigger mistake to agree to stay on until after Natalia's opening.'

'So why *did* you agree to it?'

'You know damned well why,' he growled. 'Because you managed to make yourself completely irresistible to my grandfather, didn't you? So that I could hardly refuse his suggestion that we hang around for a few more days.' His fingers tightened around his car keys as he glared at her. 'Was this just more of the same kind of behaviour you demonstrated so perfectly at your sister's wedding? Manipulating events so they'd turn out the way you wanted them to?'

'That is an outrageous thing to say,' she retorted, wrapping the duvet more tightly around herself and trying very hard to keep the sight of her tightening nipples away from his accusing eyes. 'Unless you're suggesting that I deliberately went out of my way to be nice to your grandfather, just because I had some sort of hidden agenda to trap you in this cottage?'

He gave an impatient shake of his head. 'That wasn't what I meant.'

'Because, believe me, no one would deliberately angle to have more time alone with you, when you're in *this* kind of mood!'

His eyes narrowed. 'I guess not,' he said.

'And to be honest, I don't know how much longer I can go on like this,' she said. 'Maintaining this crazy fiction of presenting ourselves as the happy couple whenever we're with Giovanni or Natalia—and yet the moment we're alone, we're...we're...'

Dante stilled as he heard the unmistakable break in her voice, which only added to his growing sense of confusion and frustration. Because he hated it when she acted vulnerable—something which was surprisingly rare. When her voice wobbled or she got that puppy-dog look in her eyes, it started making all kinds of unwanted ideas flood into his head. Was it possible that duplicity didn't come as easily to her as he'd originally thought? That the sweet and uncomplicated Willow he'd seen here in his Long Island home—being endlessly patient with his grandfather and lovely towards his sister—was actually the real Willow? His mouth hardened. Or was she trying and managing very successfully to twist him around her little finger?

'We what, Willow?' he questioned silkily.

'We circle each other like two wary animals whenever we're together!'

'Well, let me ease the burden by going out and making sure we're alone for as little time as possible,' he said. 'Like I said, I'm going out for a drive. I'll see you later.'

Walking across the room, he clicked the door shut behind him, and as Willow listened to the sound of his retreating footsteps, she slumped dejectedly back into the pillows.

A heavy sigh escaped from her lips. She was living in a prison. A gilded prison where everything she wanted was right in front of her. The only man she'd ever wanted was constantly within touching distance—only she wasn't allowed to touch. And the fiction of the happy front they presented to the outside world was cancelled out by the spiralling tension whenever they were alone together.

She'd thought she'd been getting close to him. She *had* been getting close to him. On the day they'd arrived, he'd dropped his formidable guard and told her things about his past—things about his childhood and his family which had made her want to reach out to him. She'd seen the bitter sadness distorting his features and had wanted more than anything else to comfort him.

And for a while he had let her. For a few moments he had held her tight and kissed her and something deep and strong had flickered into life as they'd stood, locked in each other's arms. Her experience of men was tiny, but she had *known* that kiss was about more than sexual desire. It had been about understanding and solace. She'd thought it had been about hope.

But then he had pushed her away almost coldly, and since then he hadn't come close. Only when they were being observed by other people did he soften his attitude towards her.

She'd met one of his sisters, Natalia—a talented artist who lived at the house. With her wavy brown hair tied back in a ponytail and tomboyish clothes, she wasn't a bit how Willow had imagined Dante's sister to be. She had recently returned from a trip to Greece, but her clear hazel eyes became shuttered whenever anyone asked about it.

And Willow had at last met the legendary Giovanni, Dante's grandfather. She'd felt a punch of painful recognition after being shown into his room and seeing the pills which the attendant nurse was tipping into a small plastic container. A sense of sadness had curled itself around her heart as she saw the unmistakable signs of sickness. She thought how the Di Sione family had so many of the things which society lusted after. With their lavish wealth and a sprawling mansion in one of the world's most expensive areas of real estate, they were a force to be reckoned with...but nobody could avoid the inevitability of death, no matter how rich they were. And Dante's grandfather's eyes held within them a pain which Willow suspected was caused by more than his illness. Was he trying to get his affairs in order before the end? Was that why he'd asked Dante to trace the costly tiara and bring it to him?

On the first of what became twice daily visits, Willow would perch on a chair beside the bed and chat to the old man. She told him all about her life in England, because she knew better than anyone how being housebound made the dimensions of your world shrink. She was less enthusiastic about her fictitious future with his beloved grandson, even though the old man's eyes softened with obvious emotion when he reached out to examine her sparkling engagement ring. And she hoped she'd done her best to hide her guilt and her pain—and to bite back the urge to confess to him that none of this was real.

After Dante had gone she lay in bed until the light came up, then walked over to the main house for breakfast. The dining room was empty but Alma must have heard her because she came in with a pot of camomile tea, just as Willow was helping herself to a slice of toast.

'Where is everyone?' asked Willow as she reached for a dish of jam.

'Signor Giovanni is resting and Miss Natalia's upstairs, trying on dresses for her exhibition,' replied Alma. 'Would you like Cook to fix you some eggs?'

Willow shook her head. 'I'm good, thanks, Alma. This jam is amazing.'

Alma smiled. 'Thank you. I made it myself.'

Slowly, Willow ate her breakfast and afterwards went for a wander around the house where there was always something new to discover. And it was a relief to be able to distract herself from her endless frustration about Dante by admiring the fabulous views over the Di Sione estate, and the priceless artwork which studded each and every wall of the mansion. She was lost in thought as she studied a beautiful oil painting of Venice when suddenly she heard a small crash on the first floor, followed by the unmistakable sound of Natalia's voice exclaiming something.

Curiosity getting the better of her, she walked up the curving staircase and along a wide corridor, past an open door where she could see Natalia standing in front of a mirror, a heavy silver hairbrush lying by her bare feet. She was wearing a green shift dress—one of the most shapeless garments Willow had ever seen—which did absolutely nothing for her athletic physique.

Instinctively, she winced and the words were out of her mouth before she could stop them. 'You're not wearing that, surely?'

'What?' Natalia looked down at the garment before glancing up again and blinking. 'This is one of my best dresses.'

'Okay,' said Willow doubtfully, going into the room and walking around behind Natalia to see if it looked any better from the back. It didn't.

'So what's wrong with this dress?' Natalia asked.

Willow shrugged as she looked at Dante's sister. 'Honestly? It looks like a green bin bag. Admittedly a very nice shade of green, but still…' She narrowed her eyes in assessment. 'Did Dante tell you that I work in fashion?'

Natalia shook her head. 'Nope. He's been characteristically cagey about you. If you want the truth, I was pretty surprised to meet you. He once told me that he didn't think that marriage was for him, and I believed him.' Her voice softened. 'That's why I'm so happy for him, Willow. Sometimes he seems so…alone…despite all the planes and the parties and the money he's made. I'm so glad he's found you.'

Willow's heart clenched with a guilt even though she felt a perverse kind of pride that their farce of togetherness was working so effectively. She turned her attention to Natalia again.

'You have a knockout figure and gorgeous hair and you don't do much with either.'

'I've never had to.'

'But today is different, isn't it?' persisted Willow. 'I mean, it's meant to be special.'

There was silence for a moment before Natalia answered. 'Yes.'

Willow glanced over at the clock on the mantelpiece. 'Look, we have plenty of time. I can see what you have in your wardrobe or we could raid mine. And I'm a dab hand with a needle and thread. Will you let me give you a bit of a makeover? Only if you want to, of course.'

There was a moment of hesitation before Natalia gave Willow the sweetest smile she'd ever seen. 'Sure,' she said. 'Why not?'

Dante parked the car and walked slowly to the house, his dark glasses shading his eyes against the bright golden glitter of the day. It was a beautiful day and he should have felt invigorated by the air and the drive he'd just had. He should have felt all kinds of things, but he didn't.

Because none of this was turning out the way it was supposed to. He'd thought that maintaining a fake relationship with Willow would be easy. He just hadn't anticipated the reality.

He hadn't thought through what it would be like, being with her day in and day out, because he had no experience of what it *would* be like. Because he didn't do *proximity*. He slept with women, yes. He *loved* sleeping with women and occasionally taking them out to dinner or the theatre—but any time he spent with them was doled out in very manageable slots and always on *his* terms. Yet now he found himself stuck with her in a cottage which seemed way too small and claustrophobic, and with no means of escape. His throat dried. She was there, but not there. She was tantalisingly close, yet he had forbidden himself to touch her, for reasons which seemed less important as each day passed. And now a terrible sexual hunger raged somewhere deep inside him and it was driving him crazy.

For the first time in a long time, he found himself thinking about his twin. Was it being back here, and seeing the great sweep of lawns where they used to climb trees and throw balls, which had made the pain suddenly feel so raw again?

He thought about what he'd done to Dario, and how he'd tried to make amends, and the taste in his mouth grew bitter. Because Dario hadn't wanted amends, had he? There was no forgiveness in his brother's heart.

Deciding to have some coffee before he faced Willow, Dante walked into the house to hear laughter floating down the curving staircase from one of the upstairs bedrooms. His eyes narrowed—the carefree quality of the sound impacting powerfully on his troubled thoughts. Frowning a little, he followed the unfamiliar sound until he reached his sister's bedroom, unprepared for the sight which awaited him.

Talia was standing on a chair, and Willow was kneeling on the floor beside it, with pins in her mouth as she tugged at the hem of a beautiful floaty dress quite unlike anything he'd ever seen his sister wear before. And it wasn't just the dress. He'd never seen Natalia with her hair like that either, or her eyes looking so big. He caught the milky lustre of pearls at her ears—

they glowed gently against her skin—and suddenly felt a surge of protectiveness, because this was his baby sister, looking all grown up.

'What's going on?' he said.

Natalia looked up. 'Hi, Dante.' She smiled. 'I'm deciding what to wear to the exhibition of my work.'

He raised an eyebrow. 'But you never go to the exhibition.'

'Not in the past. But tomorrow night I do,' she said softly. 'And Willow has helped me choose what to wear. Isn't she clever?'

Willow.

For the first time, Dante allowed his gaze to linger on the slim blonde scrambling to her feet, her cheeks slightly pink as she removed a pin from her mouth and dropped it into a little pewter box. Her dress was creased and her legs were bare and he was hit by a wave of lust so powerful that he could feel all the blood drain from his head, to go straight to where his body was demanding it.

He'd left their suite early because he'd felt as if he would *explode* if he didn't touch her, and suddenly he began to wonder just what he was doing to himself. Whether pain was such an integral part of his life that he felt duty-bound to inflict it on himself, even when it wasn't necessary. Was he trying to punish himself by denying himself the pleasure which he knew could be his, if only he reached out and took it? Because Willow hungered for him, just as much as he did for her. He could read it in every movement of her body. The way her eyes darkened whenever she looked at him.

Her carelessness had led to that crazy announcement about them being engaged, but hadn't he committed far graver sins than that? Hadn't he once told the biggest lie in the world to his twin brother—a lie by omission. He had stood silent when Dario had accused him of sleeping with his wife, and hadn't their relationship been in tatters ever since?

Pushing away the regret which he'd buried so

deep, he thought instead about what his grandfather had said, soon after he'd given him the tiara. That Willow was caring and thoughtful, and that he liked her. And Giovanni wouldn't say something like that unless he meant it. His sister seemed to like her too—and Talia could be notoriously prickly with new people, after all the bad stuff which had happened in *her* life.

He realised that Natalia was waiting for an answer to a question he'd forgotten. Something about Willow, he thought—which was kind of appropriate because it was difficult to concentrate on anything other than a pair of grey eyes and a soft pair of lips he badly needed to kiss.

'Yes, she is,' he said slowly. 'Very clever.'

A funny kind of silence descended as Willow's cheeks grew pink.

'Well, I think that's everything,' she said, brushing her hand down over the creases in her dress. 'You look gorgeous, Natalia.'

'Gorgeous,' Dante agreed steadily. 'And now

I'd like to talk to you, Willow. That is, if Natalia has finished with you.'

'Sure.' Natalia gave a quick smile. 'We're all done here.'

In silence Dante followed Willow from Natalia's room, and once he had closed the door, she turned to him, her eyes filled with question.

'What is it?' she asked. 'Has something happened?'

But he shook his head. He didn't want whispered explanations in the corridors of this great house, with Natalia suddenly emerging from the bedroom or Alma or another member of staff stumbling upon them. He badly wanted to kiss her, and once he'd started, he wasn't sure that he'd be able to stop.

'I need to talk to you,' he said. 'In private.'

The journey to their cottage seemed to take for ever, and Willow's heart was pounding as she followed Dante through the grounds because she was aware that something about him was different. When he'd walked into the room and seen her and Natalia giggling together, there had been something in his eyes which had made her want to melt. He'd looked at her in a way which had made goose bumps whisper all over her skin and her heart start thumping with an urgent kind of hope. She'd seen a new tension in his body and hoped she hadn't imagined the hunger she'd seen in his blue eyes, but even if it was true, she wasn't sure she trusted it. Was he going to take her in his arms and run his hands over her body like he'd done before? Was he going to kiss her passionately—to the point where she was gasping with hunger and frustration—only to push her away again and add to that frustration?

In tense silence they walked down an avenue of tall trees, whose leaves were brushed with the first hints of gold, and when finally they reached the cottage, she turned to face him as he closed the door.

'What is it?' she questioned again. 'Why are you acting like this?'

'I'm not acting,' he said unsteadily. 'Up until

now, maybe—but not any more. I've wanted you for so long and I've reached a point where I can't go on like this any longer because it's driving me insane. I've tried to resist you, but it seems I can't resist any more. And now I'm through with trying. I want you, Willow. I want you so badly I can hardly breathe.'

Her heart was performing somersaults as she looked at him, scarcely able to believe what she was hearing. 'You make it sound as if you're doing something you don't want to do.'

'Oh, I want to do it, all right,' he said simply. 'I can't remember ever wanting a woman as much as I do right now. Maybe because you've been off-limits for so long that it's stirred my appetite until I can think of little else but you. I don't know. All I know is that I don't want to hurt you.'

'Dante…' she said.

'No. Hear me out, because it's important that you do.' His gaze was very intense—his eyes like blue flames which burned right through her. 'I'm afraid your innocence will make you read too much into this and so I'm flagging it up before that happens. To make sure it doesn't happen. Because the act of sex can be deceptive, Willow. The words spoken during intimacy can often mimic the words of love and it's important you recognise that.'

She dug her teeth into her bottom lip. 'And you're afraid that if I have sex with you, I'll fall hopelessly in love with you?'

His face became shuttered. 'Will you?'

Willow wondered if it was arrogance which had made him ask that—or simply a remarkable honesty. She wondered if she should listen to the voice inside her head which was telling her to heed his warning. That maybe she was setting herself up for a hurt bigger than any she'd ever known.

But it wasn't as easy as that. She wanted Dante in a way she'd never wanted anyone—a way she suspected she never would again. Even if she met someone else like him—which was doubtful—

her fate was always going to be different from other women her age.

Because a normal life and marriage had never been on the cards for her and it never could.

But none of that was relevant now.

She wasn't asking the impossible. She wasn't demanding that he *love* her—all she needed to do was to keep her own emotions in check. *She had to.* Because anything else would frighten him away—instinct told her that. She gave a little shrug.

'I'll try my very hardest not to fall in love with you,' she said lightly.

'Good. Because there isn't going to be some fairy-tale ending to this. This fake engagement of ours isn't suddenly going to become real.'

'I don't care.'

And suddenly neither did he. He didn't care about anything except touching her like he'd wanted to do for so long.

Dante peeled the dress from her body and then couldn't stop staring—as if it was the first time he'd ever undressed a woman. She was all sweetness and delicacy. All blond hair and floral scent and pure white lingerie. He wrapped his arms around her. He wanted to ravish her and protect her. He wanted to spill his seed inside her—and yet surely a virgin of her stature could not take him when he was already this big and this hard.

He brushed a lock of hair away from the smoothness of her cheek. 'I'm afraid I might break you.'

'You won't break me, Dante. I'm a woman, not a piece of glass.' Her voice trembled a little as she lifted her chin and he saw the sudden light of determination in her eyes. 'Don't be different towards me just because I've never done this before, or because once I was sick. Be the same as you always are.'

'Be careful what you wish for.' With a little growl, he picked her up and carried her into the bedroom. Carefully, he laid her down on the bed before moving away and beginning to unbutton his shirt, telling himself that if she looked in any way daunted as he stripped off, then he would stop.

But she was watching him like a kid in a candy store and her widened eyes and parted lips were only adding to his desire—if such a thing was possible. He eased the zip down over his straining hardness and carefully watched her reaction as he stood before her naked—but her face was full of nothing but wonder, and hunger.

'Oh, Dante,' she said, very softly.

It was the sweetest thing he'd ever heard. He went over to the bed and bent over her, tracing the pad of his thumb over her trembling lips and following it with the slowest, deepest kiss imaginable. It made his heart kick and his groin throb, and when he drew back he could see she looked dazed. *You and me both, sweetheart*, he thought, his fingertip stroking along the delicate lace of the bra which edged her creamy skin, and he felt her tremble.

'Scared?' he said.

She gave a little shrug. 'Scared I might not meet your expectations.'

He unclipped the front clasp of her bra, so that her delicious little breasts sprang free and he smiled as he bent his head to trace each budding nipple with his tongue.

'You already have,' he murmured throatily. 'You're perfect.'

Willow didn't react to that because she knew she wasn't. Nobody was and in her time she had felt more imperfect than most. But the look on his face was making her feel pretty close to perfect and she would be grateful to him for ever for that.

And now his thumbs were hooking into the sides of her knickers and he was sliding them all the way down her legs.

'Mmm…' he said, his gaze pausing to linger on her groin. 'A natural blonde.'

And Willow did something she'd never imagined she'd do on her long-anticipated initiation into sex. She burst out laughing.

'You are outrageous,' she said as he dropped the discarded underwear over the edge of the bed.

'But you like me being outrageous, don't you, Willow?'

And that was the thing. She did. Dante Di Sione was both arrogant and outrageous, yes. She could understand why they called him a maverick. But he was a lot of other things too. Most men in his position, she suspected, would have bedded her before now—but Dante had not. He had tried to do the right thing, even though it had gone against all his macho instincts. He had resisted and resisted until he could resist no more. He was strong and masterful, yet he had a conscience which made her feel safe. And safety had always been a big deal for her.

'I think you know the answer to that question,' she murmured as she tipped her head back so that he could kiss her neck.

And Dante did know. He gave a groan of satisfaction as he explored her. He touched her wetness until she was trembling uncontrollably—

until she had begun to make distracted little pleas beneath her breath. She was so ready, he thought, his heart giving a thunder of expectation as his hand groped blindly towards the bedside locker.

Thank God for condoms, he thought—though as he rolled the contraceptive on, it was the only time she seemed uncertain. He saw her biting down on her lip and he raised his eyebrows, forcing himself to ask the question, even though he could barely get the words out.

'It won't be easy and I can't promise that it won't half kill me to do it, but if you want to change your mind...'

'*No,*' she said fiercely, her eager kisses raining over his eyelids, his jaw and his mouth. 'Never! Never, never, never.'

Her eagerness made him smile and when finally he entered her there was only the briefest moment of hesitation as he broke through her hymen, and he was filled with a powerful sense of possession.

'Does it hurt?' he said indistinctly, fighting

against every instinct in his body as he forced himself to grow still inside her.

But she shook her head. 'It feels like heaven,' she said simply.

Dante closed his eyes and finally gave himself up to the rhythm which both their bodies seemed to be crying out for, though already he could sense she was very close to the edge.

Gripping her narrow hips he brought himself deeper inside her, bending his head to let his tongue flicker over her peaking nipples while she twisted like some pale and beautiful flower beneath him.

'Dante,' she gasped, but she didn't need to tell him what he already knew.

He had watched with rapt fascination the build-up of tension in her slender frame. The darkening of those wintry eyes. The way her head moved distractedly from side to side so that her hair fanned the pillow like a silky blond cloud. Her back began to arch and her legs to stiffen, and just as her body began to convulse helplessly around him, he saw the rosy darkening of her skin above her tiny breasts.

'Dante,' she gasped again, and mumbled something else, but he didn't know what it was, and frankly, he didn't care. Because he'd been holding off for so long that he couldn't endure it for a second longer, so that when eventually his orgasm came, he felt the rush of blood and pleasure as his senses began to dissolve—and he felt like he was floating.

CHAPTER TEN

TO WILLOW, IT felt like living in a dream.

Dante Di Sione was her lover and he couldn't seem to get enough of her. And the feeling was mutual.

But it wasn't a dream. It was real. She needed to remember that. To remind herself that this was temporary. That it meant nothing. It meant nothing but sex. *He'd told her that himself.*

She pulled the rumpled sheet over her and listened to the sound of running water coming from the en-suite bathroom.

The trouble was that when you really wanted something it was easy to start constructing fantasies—the kind of fantasies which had got her into trouble in the first place. She started thinking about Dante's lifestyle. About his dislike of weddings and expressed distaste of settling down and doing the 'normal' stuff. What would he say if she told him she didn't care about all that stuff either? And that they might actually be a lot more compatible than he thought.

But thinking that way could lead to madness. It could make you start hoping for the impossible—and hope was such a random and unfair emotion. Hadn't she watched her young friends die in hospital and vowed that she would never waste her time on useless hope?

So just enjoy what you have, she told herself fiercely. *Store it all up in your mind and your heart—so that you can pull it out and remember it when you're back in England and Dante Di Sione is nothing but a fast-fading memory.*

It started to feel like a real holiday as he showed her around his home territory and introduced her to places he'd grown up with. He took her to tiny restaurants in New York's Little Italy, where the maître d' would enquire after his grandfather's health and where Willow ate the best pasta of her life. They spent a day at a gorgeous place in Suffolk County called Water Mill, where a friend of Dante's had the most beautiful house, surrounded by trees. They visited Sag Harbor and spent the night having sex in a stunning hotel overlooking the water, and the following day took a trip out on the Di Sione boat, which was anchored offshore. But when she told him she wanted to see the guidebook stuff as well, he took her to Manhattan and Staten Island, to Greenwich Village and Gramercy Park—where the beautiful gardens reminded her of England. And when he teased her about being such a *tourist*, he couldn't seem to stop kissing her, even though the wind blowing off the Hudson River had felt icy cold that day.

'What are you smiling about?' questioned Dante as he came in from the shower, rubbing his hair dry.

Willow shifted a little on the bed. It was weird how your life could change so suddenly. One minute she'd been someone who knew practically nothing about men—and the next she was someone watching as one headed towards her, completely naked.

Don't get used to it, she thought. *Don't ever get used to it.*

'My thoughts are my own,' she said primly.

'I suspect you were thinking about me,' he drawled. 'Weren't you?'

'That's a very…' His shadow fell over the bed and she looked up into the glint of his blue eyes. 'A very arrogant assumption to make.'

He bent to trace a light fingertip from nipple to belly button, weaving a sensual path which made her shiver. 'But you like my arrogance,' he observed.

Willow shrugged as guilty pleasure washed over her. 'Sometimes,' she murmured. 'I know I shouldn't, but I do.'

I like pretty much everything about you.

He smiled as he sat down on the edge of the bed and slid his hand between her legs.

'What are you doing?' she said.

'I think you know the answer to that question very well, Willow Hamilton.'

She tried telling herself not to succumb as he began to move his fingers against her, because surely it would be good to turn him down once in a while? But she was fighting a losing battle. She couldn't resist him when he started to touch her like that. Or when he brushed his lips against her neck. And suddenly it was not enough. It was never enough. 'Come back to bed,' she whispered.

'I can't. I'm expecting a call from Paris. There isn't time.'

'Then make time.'

'And if I say no?'

'You'll say yes in the end, you know you will.'

Dante laughed softly as he lay down beside her, smoothing his hands over her body as he drew her close. He stroked her breasts and her belly. He brushed his lips over her thrusting nipples and the soft pelt of hair between her thighs. For a while the room was filled with the sounds of breathing and kissing and those disbelieving little gasps she always gave when she came and then in the background the sound of his work phone ringing.

'I'll call them back later,' he murmured.

Afterwards he fought sleep and dressed, though he had to resolutely turn his back on her, for fear she would delay him further. He pulled on a shirt and began to button it, but his thoughts were full of her and he didn't want them to be. He'd told himself time and time again that now Talia's show was over, he needed to finish this. To let Willow go as gently as possible and to move on. It would be better for her. Better for both of them. He frowned. So what was stopping him?

He kept trying to work out what her particular magic was, and suddenly the answer came to him. Why he couldn't seem to get enough of her.

It was because she made him feel special.

And he was not.

He was not the man she thought him to be.

He stared out of the window at the lake and felt

the swell of something unfamiliar in his heart. Was this how his twin had felt when he'd met Anais—the sense of being poised on the brink of something significant, something so big that it threatened to take over your whole life?

'Dante, what is it?' Willow was whispering from over on the bed, her brow creased. 'You look as if you've seen a ghost.'

He turned around to face her. Perhaps he had. The ghost of his stupid mistake, which had led to the severing of relations with his twin brother.

He shook his head. 'It's nothing.'

But she was rising from the rumpled sheets like a very slender Venus, her blond hair tumbling all the way down her back as she walked unselfconsciously across the room and looped her arms around his neck.

'It's clearly something,' she said.

And although she was naked and perfectly poised for kissing, in that moment all Dante could see was compassion in her eyes and his instinct was to turn away from her. Because all his life he'd run from compassion…a quality he'd always associated with pity, and he was much too proud to tolerate *pity*—he'd had enough of that to last a lifetime. He'd seen it on the faces of those well-meaning psychologists his grandfather had employed after the fatal crash which had left them all orphaned. He'd seen it etched on the features of those matrons at boarding school, where they'd been sent when Giovanni had finally admitted he couldn't cope any more. They'd all tried to get him to *talk* about stuff and to tell them how he *felt*. But he had clammed up, like those mussels he sometimes ate with frites in France—the ones with the tight shells you weren't supposed to touch.

Yet something about Willow made him want to talk. Made him want to tell her everything.

'You know I have a twin brother?' he said suddenly.

Cautiously, she nodded. 'But you don't talk about him.'

'That's because we are estranged. We haven't spoken in years.'

He untangled her arms from his neck and walked over to the bed, picking up a flimsy silk wrap and throwing it to her, disappointed yet relieved when she slipped it on because he couldn't really think straight when she was naked like that.

He drew in a deep breath as he met the unspoken question in her eyes. 'The two of us were sent away to a fancy boarding school in Europe,' he said slowly. 'And after we left, we started up a business together—catering for the desires of the super-rich. Our motto was *"Nothing's impossible,"* and for a while nothing was. It was successful beyond our wildest dreams…and then my brother met a woman called Anais and married her.'

There was a pause. 'And was that so bad?'

Dante looked into her clear grey eyes and it was as if he'd never really considered the matter dispassionately before. 'I thought it was,' he said slowly. 'I was convinced that she wanted Dario's ring on her finger for all the wrong reasons. Women have always been attracted to the Di Sione name in pursuit of power and privilege. But in Anais's case, I thought it was for the sake of a green card. More than that, I could see that she had her hooks into my brother. I could tell he really cared about her—and I'd never seen him that way before.'

'So what happened?' she said, breaking the brittle silence which followed.

Dante met her eyes. He had done what he had done for a reason and at the time it had seemed like a good reason, only now he was starting to see clearly the havoc he had wrought. He suddenly realised that his dislike of his twin's wife went much deeper than suspecting she just wanted a green card.

'I didn't trust her,' he said. 'But then, I didn't trust any woman.'

'Why not?'

'It's complicated.'

'Life is complicated, Dante.'

His mouth twisted. 'It's not a story I'm particularly proud of, but when we were at college, I was sleeping with a woman called Lucy. She was quite something. Or at least, so I thought—until I discovered she'd been sleeping with my twin brother as well.'

Willow stared at him. 'That's terrible,' she whispered.

He shrugged. 'I laughed it off and made out like it didn't matter. But it did. Maybe it turned her on to have sex with two men who looked identical. Or maybe she was just after the family name and didn't care which brother should be the one to give her that name.' He hesitated. 'All I know is that, afterwards, things were never quite the same between me and Dario. Something had come between us, though neither of us acknowledged it at the time. And after that, I always viewed women with suspicion.'

'I suppose so,' said Willow, and her hand reached up to touch his jaw. 'But after what had happened, it was natural you would be suspicious and examine the motives of the woman he eventually married. You were obviously looking out for him—you shouldn't beat yourself up about it.'

But Dante shook his head, forcing himself to look at the situation squarely for the first time. To see things as they were and not how he'd wanted them to be. And Willow needed to hear this. He didn't want her building up fantasies about him being the kind of caring brother who was just looking out for his twin. She needed to hear the truth.

'It wasn't just that,' he admitted slowly. 'The truth was that I wasn't crazy about Dario's new wife. I didn't like the power she had once she had his ring on her finger. She was so damned... *opinionated* and I hated the way Dario started listening to her, instead of me. Maybe I was just plain jealous.' He gave a ragged sigh. 'When he was out one morning I went round to confront Anais about her real motives in marrying him. I accused her of using him to get herself a green card and we had one hell of a row, which ended up with her throwing a glass of water over me. I guess I deserved it. We both backed down and that might have been the end of it—in fact, we'd both started talking—had Dario not walked in and found me walking out of *his* bedroom, buttoning up one of *his* shirts. He thought we'd been having sex.' He looked into Willow's widened eyes. 'He asked whether we'd been having sex.'

'And what...what did you say?'

'I didn't,' said Dante slowly. 'I didn't say anything. I used my silence to allow him come to his own conclusions, only they were the wrong conclusions. Because even though we'd both slept with Lucy, there was no way I would have ever touched his wife. But that didn't matter. All that mattered was that I felt this fierce kind of anger that he had accused me of such a thing. I thought that their relationship couldn't be so great if he thought his wife would jump straight into bed with his brother at the first opportunity. I thought the only way for things to get back to normal

would be for them to break up—and they did.
The marriage imploded and Dario cut all ties
with me. He held me responsible and I couldn't
blame him for that.'

'And did you...did you ever try to make amends?'

He nodded. 'At first I did. I was eaten up with
guilt and remorse. But no matter how many times
I tried to contact him, his mind was made up and
he wouldn't see me, or speak to me. It was like
trying to smash my way through a concrete wall
with nothing but my bare hands, and in the end
I gave up trying.'

He waited for her judgement. For the shock and
outrage he would expect from a woman whose
innocence he had taken and whose total tally of
sexual partners was just one. Wouldn't she be
disgusted by what he had done? Wouldn't she
want to walk away from him, no matter how
good he was between the sheets?

But there was no judgement there. The concern had not left her eyes. And for the first time
in his life he was finding compassion tolerable.

'Why don't you go to him?' she asked.

'Because he won't see me.'

'Couldn't you at least...*try*? Because...' She sucked in a deep breath. 'The thing is, Dante... one thing I learnt when I was so ill was just how important family are. They should be the people you can depend on, no matter what. And you never, ever know what's around the corner. If something happened to Dario and you were still estranged, you'd never forgive yourself. Would you? And it's not too late to try again.' Her words became urgent. 'It's *never* too late.'

He shook his head, because hadn't he grown weary with being stonewalled? And all these years down the line, surely rejection would be all the harder to take. But as Dante looked into Willow's face, he realised he needed to be bigger than his pride and his ego. He thought about all the things she'd been through—things she hadn't wanted to tell him but which eventually he'd managed to prise from her. He thought about how she'd minimised her sickness with a few flippant sentences, making it sound no more inconvenient than a temporary power cut. Despite her slight frame and ethereal appearance, she was brave and resilient and he admired her for those strengths.

Walking over to the writing desk, he picked up his phone, but when he saw the name which had flashed onto the screen, he felt a sense of disbelief as he scrolled down to read the message. He looked up, to where Willow hadn't moved, a question darkening her grey eyes.

'What's wrong?'

'It's from Dario,' he said incredulously. 'And he wants to meet me.'

Her expression echoed his own disbelief. 'Just like that? Right out of the blue? Just after we'd been talking about him?'

'He says he heard I was at the house and decided to contact me.'

She gave a slightly nervous laugh. 'So it's just coincidence.'

'Yeah. Just coincidence.' But Dante found himself thinking about something he hadn't allowed himself to think about for a long time. About the intuition which had always existed between Dario and him—that mythical twin intuition which used to drive everyone crazy with frustration. They'd used it to play tricks on people. They'd loved making their teachers guess which twin they were talking to. But there had been another side too. The internal side which had nothing to do with playacting. His pain had been his brother's pain. Their joy and dreams had been equally shared, until a woman had come between them.

And maybe that was how it was supposed to be. Maybe he had wasted all that energy fighting against the inevitable. For now he could see that not only had he been jealous of Anais, he'd been angry that for once in his life he'd been unable to control the outcome of something he wanted. Because the little boy who'd been unable to save his mother had grown into a man with a need to orchestrate the world and the way it worked. A man who wanted to control people and places and things. And life wasn't like that. It never could be.

He looked at Willow and once again felt that strange kick to his heart. And even though part of him wanted to act like it wasn't happening, something was stubbornly refusing to let him off the hook so easily. Was it so bad to acknowledge the truth? To admit that she made him feel stuff he'd never felt before—stuff he hadn't imagined himself *capable* of feeling. That she had given him a flicker of hope in a future which before had always seemed so unremittingly dark?

'What does your brother say?' she was asking.

'That he wants to meet me.'

'When?'

'As soon as possible. He lives in New York. I could leave right away.'

'Then shouldn't you get going?'

The words were soft, and the way she said them curled over his skin, like warm smoke. Smoky like her eyes. He wanted to take her back to bed.

To forget all about the damned text and touch her until he was drowning in her body and feeling that strange kind of peace he felt whenever they were together, but he knew he couldn't. Because this meeting with Dario was long overdue. The rift was as deep as a canyon, and he needed to address it. To face it and accept the outcome, whatever that might be, and then go forward.

'I shouldn't be more than a few hours,' he said.

'Take as long as you like.'

His eyes narrowed. She was giving him a permission he hadn't asked for and his default setting would usually have kicked against her interference. Because he hated the idea of a woman closing in on him…trapping him…trying to get her claws hooked right into him. Yet he would have welcomed Willow clawing him—raking those neatly filed fingernails all the way down his back and making him buck with pleasure.

He wondered when it was that his opinion of her had changed so radically. When he'd realised she wasn't some overprivileged aristocrat who wanted the world to jump whenever she snapped her pretty fingers—but someone who had quietly overcome her illness? Or when she'd offered him her body and her enduring comfort, despite his arrogance and his hard, black heart?

He walked across to her. The morning sun was gilding her skin and the silky nightgown she wore was that faded pink colour you sometimes found on the inside of a shell. She looked as pink and golden as a sunrise and he put his arms around her and drew her close.

'Have I told you that every time I look at you, I want you?' he said unevenly.

'I believe you said something along those lines last night.'

He tilted up her chin with the tip of his finger. 'Well, I'm telling you again, now—only this time it's not because I'm deep inside your body and about to explode with pleasure.'

Her lips parted. 'Dante…'

He nuzzled his mouth against her neck, before drawing back to stare into her clear eyes, knowing now of all the things he wanted to say to her. But not now. Not yet. Not with so much unfinished business to attend to. 'Now kiss me, Willow,' he said softly. 'Kiss me and give me strength, to help get me through what is going to be a difficult meeting.'

CHAPTER ELEVEN

AFTER DANTE HAD gone Willow tried to keep herself busy—because it was in those quiet moments when he wasn't around that doubts began to crowd into her mind like dark shadows. But she wasn't going to think about the future, or wonder how his Manhattan meeting with his twin brother was going. She was trying to do something she'd been taught a long time ago. To live in the day. To realise that this day was all any of them knew for sure they had.

She set off for a long walk around the grounds, watching the light bouncing off the smooth surface of the lake. The leaves were already on the turn and the whispering canopies above her head hinted at the glorious shades of gold and bronze to come. She watched a squirrel bounding along a path ahead of her and she listened to the sound of birdsong, thinking how incredibly peaceful it was here and how unbelievable it was to think that the buzzing metropolis of the city was only a short distance away.

Later she went to the library and studied row upon row of beautifully bound books, wondering just how many of them had actually been read. She found a copy of *The Adventures of Huckleberry Finn* and settled down to read it, soon finding herself engrossed in the famous story and unable to believe that she'd never read it before.

The hours slid by and she watched the slanting sunlight melt into dusk and shadows fall across the manicured lawns. As evening approached, Alma came to find Willow to tell her that Giovanni was feeling well enough to join her downstairs for dinner.

It was strangely peaceful with just her and Dante's grandfather sitting there in the candlelight, eating the delicious meal which had been brought to them. The old man ate very little, though he told Willow that the tagliatelle with truffle sauce was a meal he had enjoyed in his youth, long before he'd set foot on the shores of America.

They took coffee in one of the smaller reception rooms overlooking the darkened grounds, silhouetted with tall trees and plump bushes. Against the bruised darkness of the sky, the moon was high and it glittered a shining silver path over the surface of the lake. All around her, Willow could feel space and beauty—but she felt there was something unspoken simmering away too. Some deep sadness at Giovanni's core. She wondered what was it with these Di Sione men who, despite all their wealth and very obvious success, had souls which seemed so troubled.

Quietly drinking her espresso, Willow perched on a small stool beside his chair, listening to the sweet strains of the music which he'd requested Alma put on for them. The haunting sound of violins shimmered through the air and Willow felt a glorious sense of happiness. As if there was no place in the world she'd rather be, though it would have been made perfect if Dante had returned home in time to join them.

She thought about the way he'd kissed her goodbye that morning and she could do absolutely nothing about the sudden leap of her heart. Because you could tell yourself over and over that nothing was ever going to come of this strange affair of theirs, but knowing something wasn't always enough to kill off hope.

And once again she found herself wondering if she came clean and told Dante the truth about *her* situation, whether this affair of theirs might last beyond their flight back to Europe.

Giovanni's accented voice filtered into her thoughts.

'You are not saying very much this evening, Willow,' he observed.

Willow looked up into his lined face, into eyes which were dull with age and lined with the struggle of sickness, but which must once have burned as brightly blue as Dante's own.

And I will never know Dante as an old man like this, she thought. *I will never see the passage of time leave its mark on his beautiful face.*

Briefly, she felt the painful clench of her heart and it was a few seconds before she could bring herself to speak.

'I thought you might be enjoying the music,' she said. 'And that you might prefer me not to chatter over something so beautiful.'

'Indeed. Then I must applaud your consideration as well as your taste in music.' He smiled as he put down his delicate coffee cup with a little clatter. 'But time is of the essence, and I suspect that mine is fast running out. I am delighted that my grandson has at last found someone he wishes to marry, but as yet I know little about the woman he has chosen to be his bride.'

Somehow Willow kept her smile intact, hoping her face didn't look clown-like as a result. She'd had been so busy having sex with Dante that she'd almost forgotten about the fake engagement which had brought them here in the first place.

And while she didn't want to deceive Giovanni, how could she possibly tell him the truth? She opened her mouth to try to change the subject, but it seemed Giovanni hadn't finished.

'I am something of an expert in the twists and complexities of a relationship between a man and a woman and I know that things are rarely as they seem,' he continued, the slight waver in his voice taking on a stronger note of reflection. 'But I do know one thing…'

Willow felt the punch of fear to her heart as she looked at him. 'What?' she whispered.

He smiled. 'Which is to witness the way you are when you look at Dante or speak of him.' He paused. 'For I can see for myself that your heart is full of love.'

For a moment Willow felt so choked that she couldn't speak. Yes, she'd once told her sister that she liked Dante and that had been true. But love? She thought about his anguish as he'd re-counted the story of his childhood and her de-sire to protect him—weak as she was—from any further pain. She thought about the way he made her laugh. The way he made her feel good about herself, so that she seemed to have a permanently warm glow about her. He made her feel complete—even though, for her, such a feeling could never be more than an illusion.

So could those feelings be defined as love? Could they?

Yes.

The knowledge hit her like a rogue wave which had suddenly raced up out of the sea. Yes, they could.

And even if Dante never loved her back, surely they could still be a couple until he tired of her.

Couldn't they?

'Your grandson is very difficult to resist,' she said with a smile. 'But he is a very complex man.'

Giovanni laughed. 'But of course he is. All Di Sione men are complex—it is written into our DNA. That complexity has been our attraction and our downfall—although pride has played a big part in our actions. Sometimes we make decisions which are the wrong decisions and that is part of life. We must accept the shadows in order to experience light.' His voice suddenly hardened. 'But I know as an old man who has seen much of the world that regret is one of the hardest things to live with. Don't ever risk regret, Willow.'

She nodded as she leaned forward to tuck a corner of the blanket around his knees. 'I'll try not to.'

'And let me tell you something else.' His voice had softened now, shot through with a trace of something which sounded like wistfulness. 'That I long to see the bloodline of my offspring continue before I die, and to know there is another generation of Di Siones on the way.' He smiled. 'I know deep down that Dante would make a wonderful father, even though he might not yet realise that himself. Don't wait too long before giving him a baby, my dear.'

It felt like a knife ripping through her heart as Giovanni's blessing brought all her secret fears bubbling to a head. Willow tried hard not to let her distress show, but she was grateful when the nurse came to help the patriarch to bed. And as she made her way back to the cottage, she couldn't stop Giovanni's unwittingly cruel words from echoing round and round in her head.

Don't wait too long before giving him a baby, my dear.

Stumbling inside, it took a few moments before she could compose herself enough to get ready for bed and to register from the quick glance at her cell phone that there was no missed call or text from Dante. With trembling fingers she put on her silk nightdress, slithering beneath the duvet and staring sightlessly up at the ceiling, as she reminded herself that he hadn't promised to ring.

She had to stop relying on him emotionally. She had to learn to separate from him.

This wasn't going anywhere.

It *couldn't* go anywhere, she reminded herself

fiercely. And sooner or later she had to address that fact, instead of existing in la-la land.

She fell asleep—her sleep peppered with heart-breaking dreams of empty cribs—and when she awoke, the pale light of dawn was filtering through the windows, bringing Dante's still and silhouetted form into stark relief.

Brushing the hair from her eyes, Willow sat up. 'How long have you been there?' she questioned sleepily.

He turned round slowly. So slowly that for a minute she was scared of what she might see in his face. Distress, perhaps—if his reconciliation with Dario had come to nothing.

But she couldn't tell what he was thinking because his eyes gave nothing away. They were shadowed, yes, but there was no apparent joy or sorrow in their lapis lazuli depths.

'I got back about an hour ago.'

'You didn't come to bed?'

She could have kicked herself for coming out with something so trite. Obviously he hadn't come to bed, or he wouldn't be standing at the window fully dressed, would he?

But he didn't seem irritated as he walked towards her and sat down on the edge of the mattress.

'No,' he said. 'I thought if I came to bed, then I'd have sex with you, and…'

'And you don't want sex?'

He laughed. 'I always want sex with you, Willow, but it's very distracting and right now I don't want any form of distraction.'

She nodded, staring very hard at the needlepoint bedspread before lifting her eyes to his. 'Do you want to talk about what happened?'

Dante considered her question and thought that of all the women he'd ever known, no one else would have asked it in quite that way. It was curious, yes—but it wasn't intrusive. She was making it plain that she could take it or leave it—it was entirely up to him what he chose to tell her. She didn't want to give him a hard time, he realised. And wasn't her kindness one of the things which kept drawing him back to her, time after time?

He sighed and the sound seemed to come from somewhere very deep in his lungs. It hadn't been an easy meeting with his twin, but it had been necessary. And cathartic. The pain of his remorse had hurt, but not nearly as badly as the realisation of how badly he had hurt his brother. And now that it was over he was aware of feeling lighter as a result.

'Not really. I'm done with talking about it,' he said, taking her hand within the palm of his own and wrapping his fingers around it. 'Would it be enough to tell you that Dario and I are no longer estranged?'

Willow nodded. 'Of course it's enough.' Her fingertips strayed to his shadowed jaw, where she felt the rasp of new growth against her skin.

'Willow, I need to talk to you.'

'I thought you just said you were done with talking.'

'That was about family rifts. This is something else.'

She bit her lip because now he sounded like she'd never heard him sound before. All serious and...*different*. Did he want to end it now? *Already?* 'What is it?' she questioned nervously.

Almost reflectively he began to trace a little circle over her palm before lifting his gaze to hers. And Willow didn't know if it was the fact that the sun was higher in the sky, but suddenly his eyes seemed clearer and bluer than she'd ever seen them before, and that was saying something.

'I'm in love with you,' he said.

Willow froze.

'With me?' she whispered, her voice choking a little.

He reached out his other hand—the one which wasn't holding hers—and touched her hair, as if he was testing how slowly he could slide his fingers over it.

'Yes, with you,' he said. 'The woman who has me twisted up in knots. Who made me do what

I told myself I didn't want to do. Who gave herself to me—the sweetest gift I've ever had, as well as the best sex of my life. Who taught me how to forgive myself and to seek forgiveness in others, because that has helped me repair the bitter rift with my brother. You are the strongest and bravest woman I've ever met.'

'Dante...'

'Shh. Who has withstood more than the average person will ever know,' he continued. 'And then just shrugged it off, like the average person would shrug off rain from a shower. But you are not an average person, Willow. You're the most extraordinary person I've ever met—and I want to marry you and have babies with you.'

Her voice was more urgent now. 'Dante...'

'No. Just let me finish, because I need to say this,' he said, his fingers moving from their slow exploration of her hair to alight on her lips, to silence her. And when he next spoke, his words seemed to have taken on a deeper significance and his face had grown thoughtful—as if he'd just discovered something which had taken him by surprise. 'I never thought I wanted marriage or a family because I didn't know what a happy family was, and I wasn't sure I could ever create one of my own. The only thing I did know was that I never wanted to exist in an unhappy family. Not ever again.' His mouth twisted. 'But somehow I believe I can do it with you, because I believe— with you—that anything is possible. And I want you by my side for the rest of my life, Miss Willow Anoushka Hamilton.'

Willow blinked her eyes, trying furiously to hold back the spring of tears as she tried to take in words she'd never expected to hear him say. Beautiful, heartfelt words which made her heart want to melt. Wasn't it funny how you could long for something—even though you tried to tell yourself that it was the wrong thing to long for—and then when it happened, it didn't feel quite real.

It seemed inconceivable that Dante Di Sione should be sitting there holding her hand, with all the restraint and decorum of an old-fashioned suitor and telling her he'd fallen in love with her and wanted her to have his babies. She should have been jumping up and down with excitement, like a child on Christmas morning. She should have been flinging her arms around his neck and whooping with joy, because wasn't this the culmination of all the hopes and dreams which had been building inside her, despite all her efforts to keep them under control?

So why was she sitting there, her heart sinking with dismay as she looked into his beautiful eyes and a feeling of dread making her skin grow cold and clammy?

Because she couldn't do it. She couldn't. She could never be the woman he wanted.

She thought about something else his grandfather had said to her last night and the wistful expression on his face as he'd said them. *Regret is one of the hardest things to live with. Don't ever risk regret, Willow.*

He was right. She couldn't risk regret—not for

her sake, but for Dante's. Because if he married her, he would have a lifetime of regret.

Yet how could she possibly convey that? She didn't want to disclose her own dark secret and have him kiss away her fears and tell her it didn't matter. Because it did. Maybe not now, when they were in the first flush of this powerful feeling which seemed to have crept up on them both— but later, almost certainly it would matter. When the gloss and the lust had worn off and they were faced with the reality of looking at the future. Would Dante still want her then? Wouldn't he long for his heart's desire, knowing she could never give it to him?

She couldn't give him the choice and have him decide to do something out of some misplaced sense of selflessness, or kindness. She had to make the choice for him, because it was easier this way. She drew in a deep breath and knew she had to dig deep into the past, to remember how best to do this. To recall the way she'd man-aged to convince her weeping parents that no, of course the treatment didn't hurt. She'd worked hard on her acting ability when she'd been sick and realised it was the people around her who needed comfort more than she did. Because in a funny way, what she had been going through had been all-consuming. It was the people who had to stand and watch helplessly from the sidelines who suffered the most.

So use some of that acting talent now. Play the biggest part of your life by convincing Dante Di Sione that you don't want to marry him.

'I can't marry you, Dante,' she said, aware that his blue eyes had narrowed. Was that in surprise, or disbelief? Both, probably. He may have just made the most romantic declaration in the world but that hadn't eradicated the natural arrogance which was so much a part of him.

He nodded, but not before she had seen that look of darkness cross over his face, and Willow had to concentrate very hard to tell herself it was better this way. That it might hurt him a bit now—and it would certainly wound his ego—but in the long run it would be better. Much better.

She knew he was waiting for an explanation and she knew she owed him one, but wouldn't all the explanations in the world sound flimsy? She couldn't say that she thought their lifestyles were incompatible, or that she'd never want to live in Paris, or even New York—because she suspected he would be able to talk her out of every single one.

There was only one way to guarantee Dante Di Sione's permanent exit from her life and it was the hardest thing to say. Hard to say it like she really meant it, but she knew she had to try.

So she made her features grow wooden and her voice quiet. Because, for some reason, quiet always worked best. It made people strain towards you to listen. It made them believe what you said.

'I can't marry you because I don't love you, Dante.'

CHAPTER TWELVE

DANTE'S EYES WERE shards of blue so cold that Willow could feel her skin freezing beneath that icy gaze. 'You don't love me?' he repeated slowly.

Willow nodded, hanging on to her composure only by a shred. 'No,' she said. 'I don't.'

She began to babble, as if adding speed to her words would somehow add conviction. 'It was just a part we were both playing for the sake of your grandfather,' she said. 'You know it was. It was the sex which made it start to seem real. Amazing and beautiful sex—although I've got nothing to compare it to, of course. But I'm guessing from your reaction that it was pretty special, and I guess that's what made us get carried away.'

He gave a short laugh. 'Made *me* get carried away, you mean?'

Keep going, she told herself. *Not much longer now. Make him think you're a cold hard bitch, if that helps.* 'Yes,' she said with a shrug of her shoulders. 'I guess.'

A strange note had entered his voice and now his eyes had grown more thoughtful. 'So it's only ever really been about sex, is that what you're saying, Willow? You decided early on that I was to be the man who took your virginity, and you were prepared to do pretty much anything to get that to happen, were you?'

All she had to do was agree with him and very soon it would be finished. Except that something in the way he was looking at her was making her throat grow dry. Because the softness had left his face and her breasts were beginning to prickle under that new, hard look in his eyes. Willow licked her lips. 'That's right.'

Dante stared at her, wondering how he could have got it so wrong. Had he been so bewitched by her proximity that he had started believing the fantasy which they'd both created? Had his reconciliation with his brother made him overly sentimental—making him want to grab at something which up until recently hadn't even been on his agenda? Perhaps his grandfather's illness had stirred up a primitive need inside him and he had made a bad judgement call. She didn't want him, or his babies. She didn't love him. She didn't care.

A smile twisted his lips. Ironic, really. He could think of a hundred women who would fight to wear his ring for real. Just not Willow Hamilton. And just because she'd never had sex with anyone before him didn't make her a saint, did it? He'd turned her on in a big way and it seemed he had liberated her enough to want to go out there and find her pleasure with other men. He felt a savage spear of something else which was new to him. Something he automatically despised because deep down he knew it would weaken him. Something he instinctively recognised as jealousy.

And suddenly he knew that in order to let her go, he had to have her one last time. To remind himself of how good she felt. To lick every inch of her soft, pale skin and touch every sinew of her slender body. To rid himself of this hateful need which was making his groin throb, even though he told himself he should be fighting it. But he couldn't. For the first time in his life, he couldn't. His sexual self-control was legendary and he had walked away from women when they'd been begging him to take them. Willow was not begging—not any more. His bitter smile returned. But pretty soon she would be.

'Well, if it's only ever been about sex, then maybe we ought to go out with a bang.' He smiled as her head jerked back, her shock palpable. 'If you'll pardon the pun.'

Willow's heart pounded as she looked into his eyes and saw the smoulder of intent there. She told herself that this was dangerous. Very dangerous. That she needed to get out of here before anything happened.

'Dante,' she whispered. But the words she'd been about to say had died on her lips because he was walking towards her with an expression on his face which was making her blood alternatively grow hot and cold. She could *see* the tension hardening his powerful body as he reached her. She could *smell* the raw scent of his arousal in the air. As he stroked a finger down over her arm, she began to shiver uncontrollably. This was wrong. It was wrong and dangerous and would lead to nowhere but pain and she knew she had to stop it. She *had* to. 'Dante,' she whispered again.

'One for the road,' he said in a cruel voice.

And then he kissed her in a way which shocked her almost as much as it turned her on. It was hard and it was masterful—an unashamed assertion of sexual power. It was all about technique and dominance—but there was no affection there.

So why did she kiss him back with a hunger

which was escalating by the second? Why didn't she just press her hands against that broad chest and push him away, instead of clinging on to him like some sort of limpet? He was strong enough and proud enough to accept her refusal. To just turn and walk away. They could end this strange relationship without stoking up any more emotional turmoil and then try to put the whole affair behind them.

But she couldn't. She wanted him too much. She always had and she always would. She wanted—how had he put it?—*one for the road.*

Did he see the sudden softening of her body, or did her face betray her change of feelings? Was that why he reached down to her delicate silk nightdress and ripped it open so that it flapped about her in tatters? His eyes were fixed on hers and she wanted to turn her head away, but she was like a starving dog sitting outside a butcher's shop as he swiftly bared his magnificent body and carelessly dropped his clothes to the floor.

Naked now, he was pressing her down against

the mattress as he moved over her, his fingertips whispering expertly over her skin, making
her writhe with hungry impatience. His big body
was fiercely aroused, and even though his face
looked dark and forbidding, Willow didn't care.
Because how could she care about anything when
he was making her feel like *this*?

She shuddered as he palmed her breasts and
then bent his head to lick them in turn, his breath
warm against her skin as she arched against his
tongue. She could feel the rough rasp of his un-
shaved jaw rubbing against her skin and knew
that it would be reddened by the time he had finished. And when he drew his head back she almost gasped when she saw the intense look of
hunger on his face, his cheekbones flushed and
his blue eyes smoky.

'Ride me,' he said deliberately.

She wanted to say no. She wanted him to kiss
her deeply and passionately, the way he usually
did—but she recognised that she had forfeited
that luxury by telling him she didn't love him.

All she had left was sex—and this was the very last time she would have even that. So make it raunchy, she told herself fiercely. Make him believe that this was what the whole thing had been about.

She slid out from underneath him to position herself on top, taking his moist and swollen tip and groping on the nearby bedside table for the condoms he always kept there. He had taught her to do this as he had taught her so much else, and she had worked on her condom application skills as diligently as a novice pianist practising her scales. So now she teased him with her fingertips as she slid the rubber over his erect shaft, enjoying his moan of satisfaction—even though it was breaking her heart to realise she would never hear it again. And when she took him deep inside her and began to move slowly up and down, he felt so big that she was certain he would split her in two. But he didn't. Her body quickly adapted to him, slickly tightening around him until she saw his fingers claw desperately at the rucked sheet on which they lay.

For a while she played the part expected of her and for a while it came so easily. Her fingers were tangled in her hair and her head was thrown back in mindless ecstasy as she rode him, glad she didn't have to stare into his beautiful face, scared that she might falter and give away her true feelings. Blurt out something stupid, and very loving. But suddenly he caught hold of her hips and levered her off him. Ignoring her murmur of protest, he laid her down flat against the mattress and moved over her again.

'No,' he said, his voice very intent as he made that first renewed thrust deep inside her. 'I want to dominate you, Willow. I want to remind myself that everything you know you have learned from me. I want to watch your face as you come, and I want you to realise that never again will you feel me doing this…and this…and *this*…'

She cried out then, because the pleasure was so intense it was close to pain. And if the first time they'd ever made love she had begged him not to be gentle with her—not to treat her as if she was made of glass—he certainly wasn't gentle now. It was as if he was determined to show her everything he was capable of, as he drove into her with a power which had her nails digging helplessly into his shoulders.

She almost didn't *want* to come—as if her orgasm would be a sign of weakness and by holding it back she could retain some control over what was happening—but already it was too late. Her back was beginning to arch, her body spasming around him as she opened her mouth to cry out her satisfaction.

But for once he didn't kiss the sound away and blot it into silence with his lips. Instead he just watched her as she screamed, as cold-bloodedly as a scientist might observe an experiment which was taking place in the laboratory. Only then did he give in to his own orgasm and she thought it seemed brief and almost perfunctory. He didn't collapse against her, whispering the soft words in

French or Italian which turned her on so much. He simply pumped his seed efficiently into the condom before withdrawing from her and rolling away to the other side of the bed.

Several agonisingly long minutes passed before he turned to look at her and something about the coldness of his blue gaze made her want to shiver again.

'Time to get on that road,' he said softly.

And he walked straight towards the bathroom without a backward glance.

Willow's hands were trembling as she gathered up the tattered fragments of her torn nightdress and stuffed them into her suitcase, terrified that one of the staff would find them. She had composed herself a little by the time Dante emerged, freshly showered and shaved and wearing a dark and immaculate suit which made him seem even more distant than the look in his eyes suggested he was.

'Are you…are you going somewhere?' she said.

'I am.' He gave a cold smile. 'I'm leaving. And

obviously, you'll be coming with me. We will drive to the airport—only we'll be going our separate ways from now on. You'll be heading for London, while my destination is Paris. But first, I need to speak to my grandfather.'

'Dante...'

'Save your breath, Willow,' he said coolly. 'I think we've said everything which needs to be said. I guess I should thank you for playing such a convincing fiancée. But I'm going to sit down with Giovanni and tell him that our relationship is over, and to remind him that he knows better than anyone that marriages simply don't work if there is no love involved.' His eyes glittered. 'If you're willing to sign a confidentiality clause, you can keep the ring. You should be able to get a decent amount of money for it.'

'I don't need to sign a confidentiality clause. And I won't talk about this to anyone. Why would I? It's not exactly something I'm very proud of.' Her voice was trembling as she stared at the huge diamond and thought about how much it must be worth. Shouldn't she keep it and sell it, and use the money to do some real good—for people who badly needed it? And wouldn't it help if he thought of her as greedy and grasping? If she could give him yet another reason to hate her? She curved her mouth into a speculative smile. 'But yes, I will keep the ring.'

The look of contempt on his lips was unmistakable as he turned away. 'Be my guest. And now pack your case and get dressed,' he said harshly. 'And let's get out of here.'

CHAPTER THIRTEEN

BEHIND THE FLASHING blue and gold illuminations of the Eiffel Tower, the Parisian sky was dark and starless and the streets were quiet. Far below the windows of his offices, the river Seine looked cold and uninviting and Dante was lost in thought when he heard the door open behind him and someone walk in. He swivelled round in his chair to see his assistant standing there, a pointed expression on his face.

'Yes, what is it, René?' he questioned impatiently.

'You are due at a drinks party at the Ritz...' René looked down at his watch. 'Ten minutes ago actually.'

Dante scowled. 'Ring them. Tell them that I've been held up and unlikely to make it in time.'

'I could do that, of course,' said René carefully. 'But it is the birthday party of the countess—and you know how much she wants you there.'

Dante leaned back. Yes, he knew. The whole world always wanted him, women especially. Except for one woman. His mouth hardened as he stared into space.

One woman. One infernal, infuriating woman who had made it clear that wanting him was the last thing on her particular wish list.

'Is there…is there something wrong, boss?'

Dante glanced across the room, tempted to confide in his loyal assistant—not something he ever did usually. But then, he didn't *usually* feel as if a heavy weight was pressing down hard on his heart, did he? Or his life seem as if there was something fundamental missing which made him feel only half complete. He shut his eyes. Had he imagined that the heartless way that the beautiful blonde had rejected him would have been enough to make him see sense? And that it would somehow be easy to forget her? Because if that was the case then it seemed that yet again he had been wrong, and he didn't like being wrong.

He thought about the contradiction she'd been. The tender and passionate woman in his arms who had rapturously embraced the joys of sex. He remembered her childlike delight when he'd taken her to Shelter Island for breakfast. The way she'd charmed his grandfather and made his tomboy sister look like a million dollars. He thought about the crazy hope she'd awoken in his heart, along with the realisation that, suddenly, all the things he'd never dared dream of felt as if they could be possible with her. He remembered the trembling expression on her face when he'd asked her to marry him. The way she'd tried to blink back the sudden tears of joy as she looked at him.

And then?

Then…nothing. In a voice which was deathly quiet and a face devoid of emotion, she had told him she couldn't marry him. She'd told him she didn't love him when those words belied her every action. It didn't make sense. He shook his head. None of it made sense. If she hadn't been so innocent, he might have suspected the presence of another man. Though maybe that wasn't such a crazy idea? She'd grabbed at the diamond ring quickly enough, hadn't she? So maybe she wasn't quite as naive as she seemed.

He watched as the lights on the tower turned to red, and then to gold. Perhaps he had been nothing but her *stud*—an alpha male chosen as the ideal candidate for her sexual initiation. Maybe the fact that he was a foreigner had allowed her to shed all her inhibitions—he knew some women were like that—when all along she'd intended to marry an English aristocrat of the same class as herself.

Once again, an unwanted streak of jealousy flooded through his veins like dark poison and he opened his eyes to find René looking at him with that same expression of concern. He thought about his assistant's question and he realised that yes, something was *very* wrong and it was more to do with his own behaviour. Because since when had he taken to asking himself questions, without bothering to seek out the answers?

'I need some information about a woman.'

'Same woman as before?' asked René innocently. 'It wouldn't happen to be a Miss Willow Hamilton, would it?'

'As quickly as possible,' said Dante impatiently.

'Bien sûr.' René's lips twitched. 'This is getting to be a bit of a habit if you don't mind my saying so, boss.'

'Well, I do mind.' Dante glowered as he stood up and pulled off his tie. 'I don't pay you to give your opinion when it isn't wanted. Have the car brought round and I will call at the countess's party for a while. And will you please wipe that smug expression from your face, because it is starting to infuriate me.'

Dante was driven to the first *arrondissement*, to the glittering cocktail party being held in one of the famous hotel's penthouse suites, but his heart wasn't in it—nor in any of the stellar guests who were present. The countess was delectable, but she left him cold—as did the other women who smiled at him with open invitation in their eyes. He endured it for a while, then slipped away—and when he arrived at work early the following morning, it was to find René already in the office, with a look of triumph on his face.

'I have the information you require,' he said.

'Go on.'

'She is living in London...'

'I already know that,' interrupted Dante impatiently.

'And she will be attending a fundraiser for the Leukaemia Society being held at the Granchester Hotel in London this Saturday.' René paused, his dark eyes hooded. 'You might also be interested to know that she has put her diamond engagement ring up for the charity auction.'

And for the first time in his life, Dante was speechless.

Willow looked up from behind the podium and for a moment there was complete silence in the large ballroom, before she spoke again. 'And that is why I consider it such an honour to be your new patron.'

An expectant hush fell over the assembled throng and she drew in a deep breath, knowing that she had to get this right. 'I wanted to give fellow sufferers hope, as well as supporting the fantastic new research which is taking place all over the world. I'm prepared to step out of the shadows and talk openly about what happened to me, instead of hiding it away. Because I'm better. And because, every day, there are more and more people like me, getting better. And I…'

Her words tailed off because, for a moment there, a trick of the light made her think she saw Dante standing at the back of the ballroom. She blinked, slightly impatient with herself. Was she now beginning to conjure him up from nowhere, so that he was about to become a constant presence in her daytime as well as her night-time thoughts?

'I…' She couldn't remember what she had been

saying and someone held a glass of water towards her, but she shook her head. She stared to where the man stood, her eyes drinking him in—registering every pore of his sensual face. It *was* him. Very definitely him. Because nobody in the world looked quite like Dante Di Sione. Tall and broad and strong and magnificent and somehow managing to dominate the entire room.

And she couldn't allow herself to go to pieces at this point. Too many people were relying on her.

She fumbled around for the words which had been on the tip of her tongue and somehow managed to produce them. 'I just want to say that I think you are all wonderful, and I'm delighted to be able to tell you that the silent auction has raised almost half a million pounds.' She swallowed, and then smiled—a big smile which just grew and grew. 'So thank you again from the bottom of my heart—for allowing me to give something back.'

The sound of clapping began and swelled, echoing loudly throughout the vast room as Willow stepped carefully down from the stage, her narrow silver dress not the easiest of garments to move around in. Now what did she do? She risked a glance to where Dante had stood, but he was no longer there and she felt her heart plummet. Of course he wasn't there! She had dreamt him up. It had been a fantasy—nothing more. Why would he be here when he'd flown straight back to Paris and they hadn't spoken since he had boarded his jet in New York, all those weeks ago?

'Willow.'

The sound of his voice was unmistakable and her knees buckled, but even though his hand was instantly on her elbow and his strength seemed to flow straight into her, she shook herself free. Because she had to learn to live without him. She had to.

'Dante,' she said, but her voice sounded faint. 'What are you doing here?'

His eyes were curious, but his tone was dry. 'No ideas?'

She licked her lips. 'You were in London?'

'And happened to be passing? Yeah, you could say that.' He gave a mirthless smile. 'Is there anywhere quieter we can go to talk?'

She knew she should tell him that no, there wasn't. She knew she ought to fetch her wrap and go outside to find a cab. Go home and forget she'd ever seen him. Her gaze travelled over his face and stayed fixed on the features she'd missed so much. His blue eyes. His sensual lips. The faint darkness which always lingered around his jaw. 'There's the hotel's Garden Room,' she croaked.

In silence they walked to the plant-filled bar, with its white baby grand piano tucked away in the corner. Dante immediately managed to commandeer a quiet table at the back of the room but Willow knew instantly that she'd made a mistake in her choice of venue. A big mistake. Because the air was filled with the scent of jasmine and gardenia—heady scent which seemed unbearably romantic, as did the soft music which the pianist was playing. And the flickering candlelight didn't help. Maybe she could concentrate on her drink. Order some complicated cocktail with a cherry and an umbrella and give it her full attention.

But Dante waved the hovering waiter away and she guessed it was an indication of his charisma that he should be allowed to occupy the best table in the place without even ordering a drink.

She waited to hear what he would say and she tried to second-guess him, desperately trying to work out the right answers to whatever he was going to say. Trouble was, he asked the last question she wanted to hear. The one question she didn't want to answer. She'd lied about this once before, but she had been stronger then. She'd been so certain it had been the right thing to do and she hadn't been starved of his presence for almost five weeks, so that she could barely stop herself from reaching out to touch him.

'Do you love me, Willow?'

She looked into his eyes—which were the colour of midnight in this candlelit room—and she opened her mouth to tell him no. But a rush of stupid tears filled her own eyes and prevented her from saying anything, and mutely, she found herself shaking her head.

'Do you?' he said again. 'Just tell me, Willow. Say it out loud. That's all I'm asking. Tell me you don't love me and I'll walk out of here and you'll never see me again.'

She tried. For almost a minute she tried. Tried to force the words out of her mouth in the same way that you sometimes had to prise a stubborn Brazil nut from its shell. But the words wouldn't come. They just wouldn't come. At least, not the words she knew she should say. The other ones—the eager, greedy ones—they suddenly came pouring from her lips as if she had no control over them.

'Yes,' she burst out. 'Yes, I love you. Of course I do. I didn't want to. I still don't want to. And I'm sorry. I don't want to mess you around and I certainly don't want to send out mixed messages. So it's probably better if you forget everything

I've just said. Because…because it can't lead any-where, Dante—it just *can't*.'

His eyes narrowed, like someone who had just been presented with a locked room and was working out how best to open it without a key. 'Do you want to tell me why?'

'Because I can't give you what you want,' she whispered. 'You told me you wanted marriage. And babies. Your grandfather told me that he longed for nothing more than to see the next generation of Di Siones.'

'And?'

'And I can't promise you that. I had…' She swallowed and licked her lips. 'I had treatment for my illness before I started my periods and they said it's possible—even likely—that I may not be able to have children.'

'But you didn't ever find out for sure?'

She shook her head. 'No. I know it's stupid, but I preferred to live in a state of not knowing. I guess I was too scared to confront it and I didn't want yet another negative thing to define me. It seemed much easier to just bury my head in the sand.' She shrugged and bit her lip. 'But I suppose that's difficult for you to understand.'

She didn't know what she had expected but it hadn't been for Dante to pick up her hand—her left hand—and to turn it over and study her palm as if he was able to read her future, before lifting his solemn gaze to hers.

'No,' he said. 'It's not difficult at all, because all of us are sometimes guilty of not facing a truth which is too hard to take. I did it with my own brother—refused to accept that my reluctance to share him was what lay at the root of our rift. But listen to me very carefully, Willow—because you're not thinking logically.'

Her blurry gaze fixed on his stern features. 'What do you mean?'

'There is *always* the chance that you or I can't have a baby. That applies to every couple in the world until they try themselves. Unless you're advocating putting all prospective brides and grooms through some kind of fertility test before they're allowed to marry?' He raised his eyebrows. 'I don't think even royal families adopt that strategy any more.'

'Dante...'

'No,' he said. 'You've had your say and now I'm having mine. Understand?'

Pressing her lips in on themselves, she nodded.

'I love you,' he said simply. 'And the past few weeks have made me realise how much. Time spent away from you has only increased the certainty that I want to spend the rest of my life with you, and only you.' He placed a warning finger over her lips as they began to open. 'With or without children of our own. Because children aren't a deal-breaker. You not loving me would be the only deal-breaker. That's the only thing which would stop me from wanting to marry you, and I'm afraid you've just signed your own fate by telling me that you *do* love me.'

Dazed, she stared at him. 'Am I allowed to say anything yet?'

'Only if you're prepared to see sense and accept my proposal—unless you want me to go down on one knee in this very public place and ask you all over again, despite the fact that you've already auctioned off the first ring I gave you?'

'No! No, please don't do that. Don't you *dare* do that.'

'So you will marry me?'

'It seems I have no choice!'

She was laughing but somehow she seemed to be crying at the same time and Dante was standing up and pulling her into his arms and wiping her tears away with his fingers, before kissing her in a way that made the last of her reservations melt away.

And when the picture of that ecstatic kiss made its way into the gossip columns of next day's newspapers—with the headline *Society Girl to Wed Notorious Playboy*—Willow didn't care. Because now she realised what mattered—the only thing which mattered. She was going to focus on what was truly important, and that was yet another thing Dante had taught her.

He'd taught her that love made you strong enough to overcome anything.

So she threw the newspaper down onto the carpet and turned to look at him, running her fingers over his olive skin and thinking how magnificent he looked in *her* bed.

Sleepily, he opened his eyes and gave a huge yawn as he glanced down at the bare hand which was currently inching its way up his thigh. 'I guess we'd better go out and buy you another ring. Would you like that?'

'I'd like that very much.'

'But not a diamond.' He smiled. 'A rare grey pearl, I think.'

'Mmm… That sounds perfect.' She moved over him, skin against skin, mouth against mouth— and ripples of desire shivered over her as she felt his hardness pressing against her. 'Just not now,' she whispered indistinctly. 'The ring can wait. But this can't.'

EPILOGUE

'COME AND SIT in the shade,' Dante said lazily. 'I don't want you getting burned.'

Willow pushed her straw hat back and smiled up into her husband's face. 'I'm unlikely to burn when you insist on applying factor fifty to my skin at every opportunity, am I?'

'True. In fact, I think you need another application right now,' he murmured, rising to his feet and standing over her. 'Come here.'

'That sounds like another excuse for you to start rubbing cream into my body.'

'You really think I need an excuse, Mrs Di Sione?' he growled, lifting her off the sun lounger and leading her inside to the air-conditioned cool of their beachside house.

Willow bit her lip with sheer pleasure as she

felt his lips whisper over her throat, thinking she couldn't remember ever feeling so happy. Or lucky. So very lucky. For the past month they'd been honeymooning in a Caribbean beach house, while nearby the crystal waters lapped contentedly against sugar-fine sands. They swam in the mornings, napped in the afternoons and took lazy days out on the Di Sione boat, which had been sailed from New York and was now anchored off the island.

They had married quietly in the small church built in the grounds of her parents' house and the building had been transformed for the occasion, discreetly bankrolled by her future husband. The badly repaired hole in the ceiling had been miraculously fixed and the air was scented with gardenias and jasmine similar to those which had perfumed the Garden Room at the Granchester on the night Dante had asked her to marry him.

'Did you like our wedding?' she questioned softly.

'I loved it. Every second.'

'You didn't think it was too quiet?'

'No. It was perfect. Just like you.' Dante unclipped her bikini top and began to skate his fingertips over her nipples. He had wanted a quiet wedding. There had still been so much *stuff* going on about Giovanni's Lost Mistresses—with his brothers and his sisters all over the place trying to find random pieces of jewellery and other stuff which had once belonged to his grandfather, and nothing completely resolved. The uncertainty about who would be able to attend and who wouldn't had made Dante decide to have the smallest of weddings, with only his brother Dario in attendance as his best man. He told Willow he planned for them to visit the Long Island estate during the forthcoming holidays, where they would have a big post-wedding party.

But he'd known all along that he didn't need pomp, or ceremony. If it could have been just him and Willow, he wouldn't have complained. In the end, he was the one who badly wanted to place a gold ring on her finger and make her his. He'd wanted to marry her more than he could ever remember wanting anything. Because she gave him everything he needed—and more.

And if she'd questioned him over and over about his need for children, he had reassured her with a certainty which went bone-deep. He'd told her that there were lots of possibilities open to them if they couldn't conceive. Like he'd said, it wasn't a deal-breaker. Until one day she'd started believing him and never mentioned it again. And if either of them had been able to see into the future, they would have seen Willow Di Sione holding two baby girls—beautiful, blue-eyed twins, just like their daddy.

Dante gave a contented sigh as he remembered back to their wedding day. Without a doubt she had made the most exquisite bride in the history of the world—with a veil which had been worn by her grandmother, held in place with the glittering tiara of white diamonds and emeralds as green as new leaves. Dario had offered her use of the matching earrings, but although Willow had been very grateful, she had declined the offer. 'A woman can wear *too* much jewellery, you know,' she'd whispered to her prospective husband—and Dante had laughed with a feeling of pure pleasure.

Her slender figure had been showcased by a pale, gauzy dress, beneath which she'd sported a garter embroidered with dramatic flames of yellow and red. And when slowly he'd been removing it on their wedding night, his hand had lingered on the raised surface of vibrant hues, which she'd so lovingly stitched.

'Flames?' he questioned with a frown.

'As a kind of homage to an earlier Dante and his famous inferno.' She smiled. 'But mainly because my life would be hell without you.'

He smiled back. 'Interesting. But I thought brides were traditionally supposed to have something blue?'

And that was when her fingertips reached up to trace over his cheeks with the most gentle touch he had ever known. A touch which had made him shiver with pleasure and count his blessings.

'Your eyes are the bluest thing I've ever seen, Dante Di Sione.' Her voice had been low and trembling. 'I'll settle for those.'

* * * * *

If you enjoyed this book,
look out for the next instalment of
THE BILLIONAIRE'S LEGACY:
A DI SIONE FOR THE GREEK'S PLEASURE
by Kate Hewitt.
Coming next month.